Murder Outside the Back Door

By

John Tommasi

Author's Note

The following is an account of the murder of a popular Salem, NH school teacher by her husband in Lawrence, Massachusetts in the mid 1990's. Except for several police officers and court officers, the names of all involved have been changed. Conversations have been recreated as accurately as possible with some artistic license, and there is significant artistic license on the musings of some individuals. The actual investigation and subsequent trial have been depicted as accurately as possible based on police reports, court records, articles from the Eagle Tribune and interviews by the author.

During the proof reading, some witnesses stated that a particular event didn't happen in the manner portrayed in the book, while others stated that it was exactly the way it happened. Any inaccuracies are mine.

The police reports were obtained as a result of a request for info in accordance with NH, RSA 91-A.

Acknowledgments

I would like to thank the following for taking the time to contribute, and be interviewed by the author: Jack McDonald, Fred Rheault, Roger Beaudet, John Macoul, Phil Smith Jr., Al Gould, and the staff of the Salem, NH Public Library, particularly Paul Giblin. Much of the information is from the Eagle Tribune and Salem Observer and the great reporting of Jim Patton, Bill Murphy, Brad Goldstein and Monique Duhamel.

A number of contributors wished to remain anonymous.

Table of Contents

Prologue

Chapter 1 The Twenty-four days of Christmas

Chapter 2 January-February, 1994

Chapter 3 Murder Outside the Back Door

Chapter 4 The Investigation: Sunday

Chapter 5 The Investigation: Monday

Chapter 6 The Investigation: Tuesday

Chapter 7 The Investigation: Wednesday/Arrest

Chapter 8 The Investigation: Follow up

Chapter 9 The Trial

Chapter 10 Epilogue

Chapter 11 Where Are They Now

Prologue

March 2, 1994
9:30 PM

"You had to do it now, at the wake? Really? You couldn't wait until after the funeral?"

Detective Phillips continued to look Anderson directly in the eyes.

"Hey Bob, if it wasn't for you, there wouldn't be a wake and funeral."

****

February 4, 1984

George Phillips had just finished his first cup of coffee when he received a call from dispatch.
"Hi Detective Phillips, there's a couple out here with their daughter, they want to report an assault."

"Thanks Christine, I'll be right there."

Phillips was a tall, steely blue eyed, old school cop who had been on the Salem Police Department for twenty years, the last five of those in detectives. He was a scrapper known for his no-nonsense approach.

As Phillips entered the lobby he introduced himself.

"Hello Detective Phillips. I'm Andrew MacGregor, this is my wife Linda, and daughter Cindy. Is there somewhere we can go talk?"

"Yes, please follow me." Phillips led them into the station and a private interview room. He then motioned everyone to sit down. He noticed that Cindy was a very tall pretty brunette with long hair and looked very much like her mother.

"The dispatcher told me that this was concerning an assault."

"Yes, an assault on my daughter Cindy by that sonofabitch Robert Anderson at the High School. He's lucky I don't go down there and..." He didn't finish the sentence.

Phillips was taken aback. He knew Robert Anderson. He was the Athletic Director at Salem High School and taught Physical Education. He was also the gymnastics coach. In addition, he was the president of the local Kiwanis and a Key Club contributor at the High School.

"Robert Anderson, the Athletic director?" Phillips asked sounding somewhat incredulous.

"Yea, that's him."

Phillips sat back in his chair and then turned towards Cindy.

"Okay Cindy, please tell me what happened and I'll be taking notes as you do."

Cindy MacGregor related the following story:

She told Phillips that she was a senior at Salem High and one of the cheerleader captains. She was walking to class after the first bell yesterday when Anderson asked her if she could drop by his office during lunch. Cindy was surprised that Anderson knew she had the first lunch period at 10:30. She said that she could.

"When I dropped by his office, he told me that he was thinking of changing the uniforms for the cheerleaders and he asked me if I would mind trying on an old uniform.

I told him not at all and I went to the girl's locker room which was right next to his office. After I put on the uniform he just walked in to the locker room. I couldn't help but wonder if he was waiting at the door looking in."

Phillips interjected at this point. "Cindy, was there anyone else in the locker room?"

"No, I was the only one."

"Alright, what happened next?"

"Well, he was looking at me and it was kind of creepy. After a while he asked me how I liked it and I said it was okay. He then came over and told me that he wanted to make sure that everything was covered up. He then asked me to turn around and then, that's when he grabbed my skirt and lifted it above my waist."

"What did you do?" Phillips asked.

"I slapped his hand away and asked what he was doing. He told me that he just wanted to see what the dolly looked like? Those are the shorts we wear under the skirt," Cindy said when she saw the questioning look on Phillips face.

"Thanks Cindy. What happened next?

"I told him that I wasn't comfortable and I wanted to change back into my clothes and go to class. I told him to get out."

"What did he do then Cindy?"

"He left and he told me not to be upset, he just wanted to make sure everything was covered and he left."

"Did you tell anyone else about this?"

"Yes my boyfriend and a couple of my best friends."

Phillips was pensive for a few moments while looking over his notes.

"Alright Cindy, there is enough here to charge Mr. Anderson with simple assault, but it makes it harder if there weren't any witnesses, especially if he gives a different version."

"Detective I believe my daughter implicitly," Andrew said starting to get heated.

"Mr. MacGregor, I have no problem charging Anderson. The problem is proving it in court beyond a reasonable doubt."

After a moment's hesitation Cindy's father said, "How about a polygraph?"

"I'd be amazed if Anderson would take one," Phillips said.

"No, I mean my daughter. How about if my daughter took a polygraph?"

"That would certainly help, but they're not always admissible in court," Phillips said.

Cindy then spoke up, "I would be fine with a polygraph."

Phillips looked at the family members and then spoke, "I'm going to interview Anderson and we'll take it from there. Once I speak to him, I'll call you Mr. MacGregor."

"Thanks Detective, much appreciated."

****

When Phillips went back to detectives he told his Lieutenant, Richard Dunn, what just transpired.

"You're shitting me. Do you know besides being the Athletic Director, he's the president of the Kiwanis and he's scheduled to present Paul Marchand with the Police Officer of the year award at a ceremony in late June?"

"What do you want me to do LT?"

"We have to let the Chief know, shit, he's in the Kiwanis too, and then we have to set up an interview with Anderson. Take George Winchell with you during the interview."

"Will do."

****

The interview with Anderson was set for the following Monday at 5 PM. This was to accommodate Anderson's school day and gymnastics practice after school.

Anderson was known to both Winchell and Phillips and Anderson knew the detectives.

After they were seated in the interview room, Phillips asked the first question.

"Robert, do you know why we're here?"

"I don't have the slightest idea."

"There's been a misdemeanor sexual assault charge brought against you by a cheerleader, Cindy MacGregor. She told us that you asked her to try on an old cheerleader's uniform, and then you walked into the girl's locker room, where she was the only person in there, and lifted her skirt above her waist. Is this true?"

"She said what?" Anderson asked incredulously.

Phillips repeated himself.

"That's ridiculous. The only part about that which is true is I did ask her to try on a cheerleaders outfit. We were thinking of changing them so they wouldn't be so revealing."

"Did you go into the girl's locker room?"

"I did, but only after I asked if I could come in and if everyone was decent, and we weren't the only people in there. There were two other girls in the locker room."

"Do you know who they were?"

"No I don't."

"So there were no witnesses."

"This is ridiculous. I can't believe I'm being accused of this. I've never had anything like this happen to me before. Where are you going with this?" Anderson asked while visibly upset.

"Where we're going is an investigation of an alleged sexual assault. If there's no evidence, it won't go anywhere."

"Bob, would you mind filling out a voluntary form telling us what happened?" Winchell asked.

After thinking for a moment, Anderson said, "I'm not doing anything else until I talk to my lawyer. This is over."

After Winchell walked Anderson to the door, he and Phillips met back in detectives.

"What do you think?" Phillips asked.

"It's going to be tough. It's a 'he said, she said' and unless there's any other evidence, I suspect this will go nowhere in court. What are you thinking George?"

"Well, Cindy is going to take a polygraph. We'll make some decisions after that."

The next morning, Robert Anderson called his lawyer, John Macoul, a prominent lawyer in Salem, NH, who was known for his proclivity of getting not guilty verdicts for his clients. Even though he was often on the opposite side of police officers in court, he was well liked and respected by the Salem officers.

On Tuesday morning, Phillips was bringing Lieutenant Dunn up to date on what transpired with

Anderson when he received a call from John Macoul. Macoul told him he was representing Robert Anderson and all further communication with Robert Anderson was to go through him.

"Who was that on the phone?" Dick Dunn asked.

"John Macoul, Anderson retained him as a lawyer and John was telling me that anything we want to say to Anderson or ask him, has to go through him."

"He got Macoul, damn he's good. Are you still planning on a polygraph for the MacGregor girl?"

"Yea, I have it scheduled for next week with George Tetreault of the Rockingham County Sheriff's office. We'll see what happens if she passes."

****

"Well how she'd do?" Lt. Dunn asked.

"She passed with flying colors. The polygrapher said there was absolutely no deception in her answers," Phillips answered

"What do you want to do?" Dunn asked.

"I think we have enough to charge him and I think we should. I spoke to Johnny Bates the juvenile officer, and he told me he's had reports that a lot of the girls at the high school really don't like Anderson and many referred to him as weird and touchy. He also heard stories that he had assaulted two other girls in a similar fashion to Cindy MacGregor, but the girls didn't want to come forward. I want to charge him Dick."

After a moment's thought Dunn said, "Give Macoul a call. Let's call Anderson in and see if he changes his story."

****

It was Tuesday, February 14 when John Macoul accompanied Anderson into the police station at 10 AM. It was February vacation week for New Hampshire schools.

Macoul began, "Why are we here? I would like to think we're here so you can apologize to my client after these allegations were made to an outstanding and respected citizen of the community."

Dick Dunn spoke up, "Hardly John, Cindy MacGregor passed the polygraph with no hint of deception. Here's a list of the questions she was asked and the answers, and also George Tetreault's report. We were wondering if your client would be willing to take a polygraph too."

"I don't believe in giving innocent people a polygraph. Besides, we won't agree to the admissibility of this in court, especially when it's given by someone who can be biased in your favor."

"Alright John, why don't you give her a polygraph with an individual of your choosing. Besides, I think we can get Judge Marshall to admit the results of the polygraph," Phillips said. Judge Bob Marshall was the Salem District Court Judge.

"Good luck on that, besides, we would never agree to the admissibility of the polygraph," Macoul answered, and after a moment's thought said, "If you don't mind, I'd like a few minutes with Robert alone."

"Not at all. We'll be outside. Call when you're ready."

When Phillips and Dunn were beckoned back in the room, they were surprised with what they heard from Macoul.

"I'd like to give Cindy MacGregor a polygraph with an examiner of my choosing."

"That's not a problem with us, but we'll have to talk to her father and Cindy first. We're viewing her as a victim and she's going through a lot. If we do agree, I'd want Phillips to be present prior to the actual test," Dunn said.

"That's not a problem," Macoul answered. "Let me know."

Authors note. Polygraphs are rarely admitted in court unless: (1) the parties stipulate to admissibility in advance of the test; or (2) when the polygraph results are used to impeach or corroborate the testimony of a witness. In the latter circumstance, the party seeking to introduce the polygraph results must provide adequate notice to the opposing party; the opposing party must be given adequate opportunity to have its own polygraph expert administer a test covering substantially the same questions; and the evidence must be admissible under the rules governing corroboration or impeachment.

****

Both Cindy and her parents agreed to the second polygraph with Cindy's father and detective Phillips present. She once again passed the polygraph with no deception indicated.

On Friday, March 2, Phillips, Winchell, Lieutenant Dunn and the Chief of Police had a meeting. At this meeting, Phillips stated that the MacGregor's were willing to go ahead with a trial and wanted Anderson arrested even in spite of Phillips telling Cindy's father that it would be difficult for Cindy. They still insisted.

"What do you think George," the Chief asked, "did he do it?"

"There's no doubt in my mind."

Both Dunn and Winchell agreed.

"Okay, I don't like it, but the girl passed two polygraphs. Do you think we can get that admitted in court?"

"The only chance we have is if Macoul calls Anderson as a witness and we can probably have the results admitted to contradict his testimony."

"Alright go with it."

An arrest warrant was signed by the clerk of courts and Anderson was arrested on Monday March 12. The Chief of Police called Attorney Macoul and Anderson turned himself in that night. He was released on PR (personal recognizance) bail.

Authors note: Robert Anderson's arrest did not make any of the local papers. When the author was researching the arrest, the entire arrest report was missing from the 1984 microfiche records. There was also no record of the arrest in the formal police log. This could have been caused by someone of authority "pulling" the records or by the records being misfiled.

****

Even though there were no articles in the local papers, it didn't take long for the news to spread throughout the school and the community. Anderson had applied for the position of principal of Merrimack, NH High School and the news reached them too.

There was no public mention of Anderson's arrest until there was an article in the Salem Observer on May 4th. The article indicated that Anderson was to face charges for simple assault. It also stated that Police allege the unprivileged touching of a female student by Anderson, however, no additional information was given beyond that. Court was set for June 6th, in Hampton, NH District Court. John Macoul had requested a change of venue which was granted.

In addition, there was a petition circulated around Salem High School which was signed by nearly four hundred students in support of Anderson. There was also a half page ad placed in the Salem Observer. The petition and ad read:

We the undersigned students at Salem High School wish to come to the aid of a teacher and good friend, Mr. Bob Anderson. As Athletic Director and Physical Education teacher, "Andy" has in some way touched all of our lives. He has indeed helped the quality of our education and has brought spirit to our school. For this, we are all very grateful.

The students who brought the petition to the Observer stated that the signatures of the students in the ad were not a judgement of guilt or innocence, but merely a show of support for a popular teacher.

When the Observer reached out to Anderson, he said that he was "without words for the show of support and student backing," he received. He declined comment on the case until after the court appearance.

The Observer also contacted the Superintendent of Salem Schools, Paul Johnson. Johnson stated that he would not comment on the findings of an internal investigation conducted by the district. He also stated, "That this is a touchy subject and a very personnel matter, and I don't want to make any statements that would injure either party."

Johnson also said he was unaware of the petition circulated by the students and could not make a statement regarding it.

****

"Salem Athletic Director Found Innocent," was the headline of the June 13th edition of the Salem Observer. The trial lasted three days and was in Hampton, NH District Court which was presided over by Judge Francis "Whitey" Frazier. Like Judge Bob Marshall of Salem, Judge Frazier was highly liked and respected by the Hampton Police.

In a criminal trial, the prosecution has to give the defense all its evidence and list of witnesses that it is going to present at the trial, especially evidence that is exculpatory in nature. This is called discovery. The defense can also depose these witnesses prior to the court date. A deposition is used to gather information as part of the discovery process and, in limited circumstances, may be used at trial to impeach a witness's testimony. Unlike the prosecution, the only thing that the defense has to present is a list of its witnesses that could provide an alibi.

As a result, the prosecution was faced with a number of witnesses that presented them with significant surprises.

In a trial of this nature, the defense has the option of a jury trial or allowing the sitting magistrate to determine guilt or innocence. The defense chose to do the latter.

Conventional Lawyer wisdom often points to choosing a jury if a case has emotional appeal, and choosing a judge if a case is complex and based on technical legal questions.

In his opening statement, Attorney Macoul told Judge Frazier he thought that the girl had made up the story to make her boyfriend, Tim Brady, jealous and once the story mushroomed, neither had any control of the situation.

To back up this claim, Macoul presented a former boyfriend of Cindy MacGregor who not only testified that she tried to make him jealous on multiple occasions, but that a friend of Cindy MacGregor told him that the cheerleaders were upset with Anderson and were spreading rumors. This hearsay testimony was allowed into evidence over the objections of the prosecution.

Anderson was the second witness that Macoul called who refuted all of MacGregor's accusations. There was another surprise to the prosecution when Anderson testified that MacGregor's current boyfriend, Tim Brady, came into Anderson's office the next day and attempted to "shake down" Anderson. Anderson alleged that Brady stated "what would it be worth to you for us not to cause problems." Anderson also testified that there were other girls in the locker room.

After Brady was called the following day to the stand to refute Anderson's testimony concerning his "shakedown," Macoul had another surprise when he called Sean Collins to the stand. Collins was the High School's Athletic Trainer who was appointed to the position the previous year. He testified that since his office was next to Anderson's, he heard the entire conversation between Brady and Anderson, including the alleged "shakedown."

When asked by the prosecution, Collins confirmed that Anderson was his immediate supervisor and Anderson was the person responsible for his performance evaluations.

Macoul's last witnesses were Ray Corliss, the high school principal, and Ray Johnson, the superintendent of schools. They appeared as character witnesses for Anderson. Both stated that he was a dedicated teacher and always put students first, and that they could never picture him doing what he was accused of doing.

In his closing statement, Macoul asked, "Should any teacher have to fear being alone with a student. Robert Anderson's life and career have been ruined by mere allegations."

Judge Frasier found Anderson not guilty.

****

In an interview after the trial, Anderson stated that it's good to see that the system works but I still didn't understand how it got so far (to trial). "It's a shame that my family had to go through this." He also said that he "wanted to thank the Salem High faculty, students, as well as the town for their support throughout this ordeal. Without that, I wouldn't have been able to go through it."

Amy Anderson, Robert's wife, was quoted as saying, "That girl put my husband through hell." Amy stood beside her husband throughout the trial and was always very supportive.

****

Anderson was dropped from consideration for the principal of Merrimack High, and after the school year, he "retired" from teaching and went into the cleaning business. He eventually purchased four ServiceMaster franchises.

There was no doubt in the mind of George Phillips that Anderson was guilty, and some officers speculated as to whether Anderson put Collins up to confirming his testimony concerning Tim Brady "shaking" him down.

****

About a week after the Anderson trial, John Tommasi walked into John Macoul's office. Like most other officers from Salem, Tommasi and Macoul were friendly adversaries.

"Tommasi, what can I do for you?"

"Hi John, I'd like to give you a check for fifty dollars as a retainer."

"A retainer for what?"

"Well, I'm thinking of getting married and if I would ever go through a divorce, you're the last person I want to represent my wife,"

Macoul couldn't help but laugh. "You're kidding right?"

"Nope, dead serious. I know you're reputation in court. It's too good."

Macoul laughed again. "Okay, deal."

They continued with small talk for a few minutes while avoiding the topic of the Anderson trial. As Tommasi was leaving he turned to Macoul and asked, "Hey

John, what's the difference between a dead skunk in the road and a dead lawyer in the road?"

"I'm sure you're going to tell me."

"Yup. There are skid marks in front of the skunk."

****

October 23 1989
8:30 PM

"I need help, my wife's been shot. I've been shot. I'm calling from my car phone. I'm Charles Stuart."

"Where are you sir?" answered Mass state police dispatcher Gary McLaughlin.

"I have no idea. We're coming from Brigham and Women's hospital. We were somewhere on Tremont street."

State Police Sergeant Dan Grabowski, who was the supervisor, picked up two phones. The first was an extension line which allowed him to listen in on McLaughlin's call, and the other a hot line to Boston Police.

Boston police officer, Brian Cunningham, was advised of the situation by Grabowski while McLaughlin continued to ask Stuart questions.

"Sir, where are you now? Can you indicate that to me?"

"I don't know, I don't know. I'm in a neighborhood. It looks like an abandoned area. My wife Carol has been shot bad. She's gurgling."

"Can you tell me where you are?"

"I don't know, I can't see any signs."

"Are you near Brigham and Women's hospital?"
"No we went straight through …"
"What kind of car do you have sir?"
"Toyota Cressida."
"Are you in the city of Boston?"
"Yes."
"Can you give me any indication where you may be, any building?"
"No."
"Okay, has your wife been shot as well?"
"Yes, in the head."
"In the head."
"Yea, I ducked down."
"How far and how long ago did you leave Brigham and Women's and what direction did you leave?"
"Two, three minutes."

Dispatcher McLaughlin then relayed this to Sergeant Grabowski who was still on the hotline to Boston Police Dispatch.

McLaughlin then turned his attention back to the caller.

"What's your name sir?"
"Stuart, Chuck Stuart. Should I try to drive up to the corner of the street?"
"Yes sir, if you can drive without hurting yourself. If you can, give me a cross street and I'll get someone there immediately."
"Okay, I got it started. I'm coming up the street, I can't read the sign."
"Okay Chuck, hang in there. What color is your car?"
"Blue Toyota Cressida."
"Is your wife breathing Chuck?"

"She's still gurgling. There's a busy street up ahead. I'm turning on to a busy street now. I recognize where I am. Should I drive to the hospital?"

"Just tell me what the street is Chuck."

"Ah man. I'm pulling over. It's Tremont Street."

McLaughlin relayed that to Grabowski who continued to relay it to Boston PD. The Stuarts were on Tremont Street about three minutes from Brigham and Women's hospital. Boston Police in turn dispatched four units to the area and two ambulances to stage nearby.

"Chuck, where are you buddy, Tremont Street and what? Chuck, Chuck, can you hear me?"

"Yea, I'm on Tremont Street in front of K…."

"K what Chuck. Chuck you have to help me buddy and we'll get assistance to you right away."

"Chuck, can you hear me?"

"Ah man, I'm going to pass out."

"Chuck, can you open the door? Can you open the window?"

"I'm blacking out."

"You can't black out on me. I need you man."

"My wife has stopped gurgling, she's stopped breathing."

"Chuck, I'm going to get assistance to you. Open the door. Talk to someone on the street. Open the door and talk to anyone who passes by."

After a thirty second pause, "There's no one by here."

"Chuck, Chuck, where are you shot?"

McLaughlin then turned to Grabowski, "He's faded out, we're getting nothing at all. I'm hearing breathing and some body movement, but he's unresponsive."

The above conversation between the State Police dispatcher and Stuart took slightly less than five minutes.

Fortuitously, within another minute, Boston Police located the Stuarts.

On the night the Stuarts were shot, the television show narrated by William Shatner, Rescue 911, was doing a ride along with the Boston Medical Services. Along with multiple cruisers that reached the scene, the ambulance that had the Rescue 911 film crew was the second one on the scene, and was able to get actual footage of the Stuarts being treated and placed in the ambulances. The first two medics on the scene were Dan Hickey and Kevin Ray. Hickey began working on Carol Stuart while Ray started working on Charles Stuart. They saw that Carol was in cardiac arrest and Charles was somewhat lucid. Carol was immediately placed in the ambulance, and they were able to get her heart beating again while attaching an intravenous drip. As Charles was being carried to the ambulance he kept asking about the condition of his wife and imploring medics to take care of his wife.

Once Charles Stuart was in the ambulance a police officer, who was helping to carry the stretcher asked, "Who did this? Did you see who did this?"

"A black man."

"One guy, two guys?"

"One guy."

"What he'd look like. What did he have on for clothing?"

"A black jogging suit."

"Did he have any stripes on it?"

"Yea, red stripes. He was tall and had a raspy voice."

"Did he have a mustache or beard?"

"I don't remember."

Author's note: The above conversation came from the Rescue 911 episode which is available on YouTube.

****

Carol was transported to the Brigham and Women's hospital and Charles was transported to Boston City hospital. While enroute to Brigham's, medics contacted the hospital and advised them that thirty year old Carol was pregnant, and in order to save the baby, an emergency Cesarean would have to be performed. The baby boy was delivered at Brigham's and Women's eight weeks premature. Charles and Carol had just been at Brigham's attending a child birthing class. Doctors and nurses were able to keep Carol alive through the operation, however, she died two hours later. The baby, Christopher, lived for seventeen days before dying from oxygen deprivation he suffered while in the womb.

While he was at City Hospital, twenty nine year old Charles Stuart kept asking about his wife. Doctor James Feldman described Charles' injuries as very serious and life threatening. He had a gunshot wound that exited his body. Stuart had significant internal bleeding and part of his liver was removed. After a six hour operation, he was in stable, but guarded, condition.

****

In the days after the shooting, the police dispatchers and personnel were inundated with praise. Mike Dukakis, the governor of Massachusetts at the time, made a personal visit to the dispatchers and handed out commendations and accolades.

Four days later, hundreds of mourners attended Carol's funeral including Charles' brothers, Mathew and Michael. Charles was still in the hospital but a eulogy written by Charles in the hospital, was read at the funeral. It began with, "Goodnight sweet Carol my love. God has called you into his hands, not to take you away from me but to take you away from the cruelty and violence that fills this world. We must forgive this sinner who did this to you, because God would too ... I miss and love you, your husband Chuck."

After Carol's funeral, all attention was directed to the Boston Police and pressure mounted to find Carol's killer. The motive for the killing was attributed to robbery since all of Carol's jewelry and pocketbook were missing. As one police spokesman put it, "This violence is an all too common occurrence in Boston, especially the Mission Hill district where it occurred."

Mission Hill is a ¾ square mile, primarily residential neighborhood of Boston that borders Roxbury, Jamaica Plain, Brookline and Fenway-Kenmore. It is home to several hospitals and universities, including Brigham and Women's Hospital and New England Baptist. It was known for its brick row houses, triple decker homes and high crime rate.

In the days that followed, the Mission Hill neighborhood was flooded with uniformed Police Officers and detectives. Boston Mayor Raymond Flynn issued a statement calling for a massive manhunt for the alleged killer. He ordered more than 100 extra police officers to comb not only Mission Hill, but adjacent neighborhoods, Roxbury and Jamaica Plain, which had significant black populations. Ray Flynn also went on television stating that

"The Boston Police would get the animal responsible for the killings." Skirmish lines were formed through vacant lots to find the murder weapon or any other evidence pertaining to the crime. Dumpsters and roofs were searched, all to no avail. Informants were squeezed and there were numerous complaints from black residents concerning the tactics of the Boston Police who were doing routine stop and frisks of anyone in the neighborhoods.

According to the Washington Post, one resident, Frederick Johnson, said it was like a police riot. Johnson said in a phone interview that he saw dozens of young and middle-aged men stopped and searched that fall.

The Post went on to say that "Playing to a fearful public, some officials began calling for the return of the death penalty in Massachusetts." Many in the media compared the case to the Central Park attack six months earlier in New York, where five black youths were indicted in the rape of a white female jogger. Despite this, nothing was learned, and other critics of the police said they weren't doing enough.

Five days after the murder, police arrested Alan Swanson, a homeless man they found squatting in an abandoned Mission Hill vacant building. At best, their evidence was circumstantial. He was six feet, had a raspy voice and they found a black jogging suit soaking in a pan of water. Despite the arrest, police still flooded the neighborhoods and the stop and frisks continued. Swanson was subsequently released on November 20th.

Finally, on December 28th, Charles Stuart identified Willie Bennett, a black man, in a line up. Bennett had a long record and was known as a "frequent flyer" amongst police. He was currently on parole and probation for the 1974 shooting of a police officer in Boston. He was also previously convicted of armed robbery.

However, on January 3rd, the shoe dropped. Twenty three year old Mathew Stuart, Chuck's youngest brother, approached police and told them that Charles committed the murder and he thought the reason was insurance fraud. Mathew stated, through his lawyer, that he didn't think it was right that Charles would accuse an innocent man.

It appears that Charles called his brother from Brigham and Women's hospital the night of the murder and told him to meet him in the Mission Hill neighborhood, which he did. After Chuck shot his wife and then himself, he gave Mathew Carol's jewelry, pocketbook, and the gun, a .38-caliber revolver, he used in the murder, and told him to get rid of them. Mathew, reportedly, threw the pocketbook, with the jewelry and gun in it, off the Pines River Bridge in Revere. Police divers subsequently found Carol Stuarts bag and some jewelry, but not the murder weapon.

Police then contacted the district attorney, Newman Flanagan, and at a subsequent press conference, Flanagan announced that he had instructed Boston Police to arrest Charles Stuart based on Mathew Stuarts confession.

Not surprisingly, the black community was outraged. Black Boston City Councilor Bruce Bolling stated that "The case did not go forward in the manner that it should have. Boston Police were too preoccupied with the story that Charles Stuart gave which is now a total fabrication, and because of that, hundreds of black males were harassed and demeaned." Miles O'Brien, a Boston news reporter, stated that, "the black community felt that Willie Bennett had been used in a very insidious way. The police believed the story because Charles Stuart was a victim and was seriously shot."

Mayor Flynn publicly apologized to the Bennett family.

****

The following morning at 7 AM, police found Charles Stuart's car abandoned on the lower deck of the Tobin Bridge which has a two mile span that connects Boston and Chelsea. The lower deck is one hundred forty feet above the water.

Later that day, a Boston Police boat, fished Charles Stuart's body out of the icy waters of the Mystic River. A handwritten suicide note was found in Stuart's car that stated, "I'm beaten by these new allegations and I'm sapped of all strength."

There were less than twenty people at his wake and funeral.

****

The Stuart case was far from over. Police delved into Stuart's background to look for possible motives. It was learned that Stuart was obsessed with money. He was the manager of an upscale furrier, Kakas and Sons, located on prestigious Newbury Street in Boston's Back Bay. His salary was over $90,000 ($214,000 in 2022 dollars). He had told friends and families that he wished Carol had gotten an abortion. He wasn't ready to be a father and wasn't happy with the loss of money they would incur since Carol was planning on taking three months off from work after the baby was born. Carol DiMaiti Stuart was a very successful tax attorney from a very proud and old fashioned Italian family. The Stuarts lived in Reading, north of Boston, and Carrol's parents resided in Medford. Her parents owned Sonny's Pizza and Subs in Chelsea.

Charles Stuart, according to family and friends, was concerned with the monetary loss, and by murdering Carol, not only would he be rid of the baby he didn't want, but would receive a $100,000 payment from Carol's life insurance policy (in 2022 dollars, that would be approximately $220,000). It was also reported that Charles was having an affair with Deborah Anderson, an employee he managed at Kaskas and Sons. Deborah admitted to being a friend of Charles Stuart, but denied any extramarital affair.

The police later learned that the murder weapon, a .38-caliber revolver, was stolen by Charles Stuart from Kaskas and Sons. George Kaskas Jr, said he forgot that the gun was in the store and checked to see where it was after Charles Stuart's suicide.

In October of 1992, the DiMaiti's filed a civil suit against the furrier citing:

"Stuart had tried but failed to obtain a gun elsewhere in the days before the shooting, and took the gun from the Kaskas fur store only because he knew that the gun was not likely to be missed due to the defendant's lax and careless handling of it."

The suit was filed in Suffolk County Superior Court by the victim's parents, Giusto and Evelyn DiMaiti, and her brother, Carl DiMaiti.

The suit was subsequently settled for an undisclosed amount and the proceeds went towards the Carol DiMaiti scholarship fund.

Twenty three year old Mathew Stuart was indicted by a Grand Jury later that year for insurance fraud and obstruction of justice. After being released on bail, he plead guilty to the charges the following year and received a sentence of three-to-five years. He was paroled in 1995.

****

On January 25 Carol's parents, Evelyn and Giusto DiMaiti, announced the formation of the Carol DiMaiti scholarship fund for residents of Mission Hill and Medford in Carol's name. By 2005, over $1 million dollars had been given to over 200 students.

In 2005, Season 1, episode 5 of the TV series Law and Order, was titled "Happily Ever After," and was loosely based on the murder of Carol Stuart by Charles.

Baby Christopher was buried with Carol and the grave stone reads, Carol and Christopher DiMaiti.

****

Willie Bennett was released from jail after Mathew Stuart's confession. He was arrested later that year for the armed robbery of a double amputee. He was found guilty and was sentenced 12 to 25 years in prison. In 1995, while in jail, he sued the Boston Police for false arrest during the

Stuart case. There was no culpability found on the part of the Boston Police and Bennett received nothing.

On October 23, 2017, twenty eight years after the murder of Carol Stuart, Willie Bennett was interviewed by Cheryl Fiandaca of WBZ news, a CBS subsidiary. At 67, he used a cane to walk in order to alleviate a significant limp. He stated that even now he still gets chills when he hears Charles Stuarts name and if Stuart was still alive, he would punch him in the mouth for what he did to him.

Bennett stated he wasn't surprised that he was arrested because he had a reputation in the projects of being a "wild one," and he admitted that he was one in his past. By 2017, he was in prison half his life and he stated that he wasn't going to do any more "silly shit" but just enjoy his children and grandchildren.

During the interview, Bennett wore a black jogging suit with red stripes.

****

There is a widely held conspiracy theory that Charles Stuart loved himself too much to commit suicide. The conspiracy revolves around "the belief on the streets" that someone in the DiMaiti family was "connected" and several "wise guys" forced themselves into Charles Stuart's residence on the night of January 3rd, coerced him to write a suicide note, and after the note was written, drowned him in the toilet bowl of his apartment. They subsequently drove his car to the lower deck of the Tobin Bridge where they threw his lifeless body into the icy January waters of the Mystic River.

Authors note: There is absolutely no evidence to support the above conspiracy theory. It is unknown if the coroner tested the water in Charles Stuart's lungs to see if it was fresh water from a toilet bowl, or the brackish water of the Mystic River.

****

The Stuart murder case not only received national attention, but also was run in some international newspapers. It was often mentioned by instructors at one of the three Massachusetts police academies as an investigative case example.

Police recruits weren't the only ones who studied the Stuart murder case. Robert Anderson took note of what he thought Stuart did right and what led him to being caught. Anderson certainly wasn't going to ever shoot himself, and he would never have told anyone. He did like the way Stuart had blamed the murder of his wife on the violence that was prevalent in Mission Hill and the surrounding area.

Author's note: The above musings of Robert Anderson is speculation on behalf of the author based on conversations with a number of other officers who took part in the investigation of the murder of Amy Anderson.

****

January 1992

Wendy Jack considered herself lucky. She had been friends with Bob and Amy Anderson since their student teaching days in 1975. The past year had been stressful, her father, who was living with her and her husband, had recently died and she was the executor or the estate. She and her husband were on vacation for two weeks in Florida decompressing and she was very comfortable with having Bob Anderson check the house when they were gone. She had given him a key and was confident that if anything went wrong, like a burst pipe, Bob would take care of it.

Nothing went awry while she was on vacation and everything was in order when she and her husband arrived home.

She had forgotten all about her Dad's .25-caliber gun that he kept in the top draw of his nightstand.

****

Chapter 1
The Twenty Four Days of Christmas

October - November, 1993

Bob Anderson was not happy. He had gotten a call from a customer saying that his cleaning crew didn't do a good job on an apartment in North Andover that had suffered some smoke damage from a nearby fire. Evidently, they could still smell smoke on a couple of chairs and a couch, and they withheld some of the payment from the insurance company. As the owner manager of four ServiceMaster Franchises, he felt that a personal visit by the owner would mitigate some of the ill will.

Robert went into the building and rang the buzzer for apartment 15.

"Who is it?" a young female voice answered.

"It's Robert Anderson from ServiceMaster. A Mrs. McEvoy called."

"That would be my mom. Please come up."

After Robert knocked on the door and saw who answered it, he was actually happy that his crew had done a bad job.

The woman was a slender brunette who was wearing a skirt that showed great legs and a figure to match. She had short brown hair and a beautiful face.

"Hi I'm Robert Anderson, but please, everyone calls me Bob"

"Hi Bob. I'm Pam and I live here with my parents. If you can be a little quiet, I'd appreciate it. My two year old is napping and my parents are out having lunch with friends."

"No problem," he whispered.

"Thanks."

"I guess my crew didn't do a good enough job."

I didn't think it was bad, but my mom can be picky."

"That's okay, I understand. The message I got was that she was unhappy about two chairs and a couch."

"Just the chairs. There's still a slight stain on one and she said she still smelled smoke in the other, but I can't."

Anderson walked over to the chairs and saw a slight stain on one and smelled them both.

"We'll get the stain out, and I guess if you take a really deep breath and hold it you can smell some smoke. I'll send my crew over tomorrow if that's alright and then I'll personally come over and check it."

"That'll be fine," Pam answered.

Robert was totally enamored by Pam's looks and the way she conducted herself.

"Will you be here tomorrow?" Anderson asked.

"Yes I will. I work in retail and don't have to work until the evening."

"Great. I'll send my crew over at 9, and then I'll come by and check around 11:30. And for all this inconvenience, let me take you to lunch afterwards."

"No really. It's no inconvenience."

"I insist."

"Well okay. My parents will be home and they can babysit my son."

"Great, I'll look forward to seeing you tomorrow."

****

When Anderson got back to his office, he spoke to one of his better workers, Bill Prince. Robert had coached Prince in Gymnastics at Salem High until Prince graduated in 1982. Bill had joined the marines and Anderson had written him a letter of recommendation. When Anderson started his own ServiceMaster business in 1990, Prince had recently been honorably discharged from the Marines and Anderson hired Prince and took him under his wing. Prince was a good worker and enjoyed what he did.

"Hey Bill, can you head over to that North Andover apartment tomorrow at nine and redo the two living room chairs."

"Yea no problem. Is that the one where the owners complained?"

"Yes. There's a slight stain on one and both still smell very vaguely of smoke. Take Jim with you too. I'll be by after you guys leave to make nice with the owners."

"Will do. And I'll make sure it's spotless and smells like a garden."

"I know you will."

****

Anderson arrived at the McEvoy apartment promptly at 11:30.

"Hi Pam, how did the guys do. I got a call and they told me it was done. "

"Yes and it looks like they did a very good job."

"I'm glad to hear that, I made sure my best crew was on it."

"Thanks, and they were very considerate. They asked if my son was sleeping, but my parents had taken him out to the playground since it's such a nice day for this time of year."

"I'm glad to hear it. I hope you're still interested in lunch?"

"Yes, that'll be fine. Where are we going?"

"How's Dylan's Bar and Grill sound?" Anderson said.

"Sounds good. I had a friend who worked there and she spoke highly of it."

"Is she still there?"

"No they moved to New Hampshire and she's working at the Willow tree in Salem, closer to home and no Mass income tax."

"I know that place, it used to be Lums on route 28."

Anderson had his car that day and not the van, which they took.

Over lunch, Anderson learned that Pam was a single mother and she and her son lived at her parent's apartment. She worked in retail and didn't make that much money and was constantly strapped for money. During lunch, Anderson asked her if she would like a second job, that wouldn't be difficult, where she could make a fair amount of money. Pam liked the idea and they made plans to have lunch again tomorrow.

****

When Anderson picked Pam up for lunch the next day, they went to another local restaurant, the airport café at the Lawrence airport where they ate while looking at the small planes taking off and landing.

Lawrence Airport, was actually in North Andover and the city of Lawrence paid North Andover property taxes. It was a small airport which was home to two flight schools that did pilot training and charters, with the occasional business jet.

Over lunch, Anderson asked Pam if she would be interested in being a "marketing specialist" for his four ServiceMaster franchises. When she voiced concerns that she didn't know much about marketing, he told her that it wouldn't be a problem and her job would involve driving around with him and going to prospective clients. He told her that a pretty woman who was dressed in a very sexy manner would do wonders for his business. He said that sex sells. She agreed to try it and they made plans to meet for an early lunch tomorrow and she would then drive around with him in the afternoon to some potential clients. When he dropped her off, he told her to wear a mini skirt, heels and revealing blouse, "sex sells" he said again.

****

The following day, Pam was picked up by Anderson and they visited a number of existing and potential clients. She accepted the job and worked about six hours per day, three days per week. He took her out to lunch on the days they were working together, and on most days when they weren't.

****

December, 1993

In early December, Anderson introduced McEvoy to his version of the twenty four days of Christmas. Anderson told McEvoy that he and his wife would give their children a gift every day from December 1st to December 24th, as a prelude to Christmas and that's what he was doing for her.

These gifts ranged from a teddy bear to diamond jewelry. In addition, he took her to a number of expensive restaurants in Boston, the ballet and a Garth Brook's concert.

Amy became aware of this and became increasing more disturbed over the relationship despite Robert telling her it was no more than platonic and he was just taking care of one of his employees.

Mary Lucas, Anderson's book keeper and family friend, also noticed the additional credit card charges and a change in Anderson's overall mood which became more brooding.

She was also confused when she asked Bob where the extra money was coming from in the account. When she asked Bob, he just said that they were payments from a new customer who always paid in cash. When she voiced her concerns about accountability and record keeping, she was told not to worry about it.

****

December, 1993

Bob Marshall had been a district court judge for twenty years and was sitting in his chambers at the recently constructed Salem, NH, District Court House. He was known as a tough, cop's judge and was highly respected by all in the police department. He was also the president of the local Kiwanis club and he wasn't believing what he was seeing. He had known Bob for over ten years. He had no choice but to call the police.

****

"Detective Rheault speaking."
"Hello Fred, it's Bob Marshall."
"Judge Marshall, how are you doing?"
"I've been better. I need to talk to you about the possibility of someone embezzling money from the Kiwanis. As you may know, I'm the president. Would it be possible for you to drop by the court and see me in my chambers?"
"Absolutely judge. I'll be right there."
"Thanks Fred, and please keep in mind, discretion is a necessity."
"Absolutely judge, I'll just let Lieutenant Dunn know where I'm going if that's alright with you."
"That'll be fine and tell the Dick I said hi."

****

It was the day before New Year's Eve and the court was relatively quiet. Dave Wajda had been the clerk of courts for over five years and like Bob Marshall, was well liked and respected by members of the Police Department and community. He showed Fred Rheault into Judge Marshall's chambers.

The judge was seated behind his desk and motioned Fred to sit down.

"Fred, do you know Bob Anderson?"

"Yes I do, he used to be a teacher at Salem High School, and if I'm not mistaken, he owns a ServiceMaster Franchise or two." Fred also knew of Anderson's arrest in 1984 for sexual assault, but said nothing concerning that.

"That's right. He actually owns several ServiceMaster franchises and he's currently the treasurer of the Kiwanis club."

"Wasn't he a past president too, I remember a couple of years he would give out the Police Officer of the year award at a ceremony."

"Yes, well I'm the president right now and I'm going to get right to the point. As the president of the Kiwanis club, I have access to all finances and as I was going over them yesterday, and then double checking this morning, it looks like we're missing around five thousand dollars, and it looks like Bob may have taken the money."

Fred nodded his head. He wasn't surprised. Despite Bob Anderson's high standing in the community, most members of the police department who were still around from 1984 felt that he was, at best, of low character.

"What do you have for paperwork judge and how long has this been going on?"

"It looks like it's been going on all year since he got in as Treasurer last January, but I just noticed it this past month when the withdrawals greatly increased. It looks like half of the five thousand was withdrawn in December before Christmas."

"Okay, how about paperwork?"

"I have all the monthly bank statements for the year and copies of every cancelled check. There are a number made out to cash, which I think represents the money Anderson embezzled, and he labeled a lot of theses as miscellaneous expense."

"What can you do Fred?"

After a moment's pause Fred said, "I think I'll run this past Sergeant Tommasi, he teaches financial accounting, and besides having his MBA, he's finishing up a second Master's degree in Economics."

"That's good. I seem to remember when he was in detectives he also did a number of cases like this."

"That's right Judge, we were roommates before I got married and he's good at this. He's working tonight and I'll run it past him. What are you going to do in the meantime so Anderson doesn't write anymore checks?"

"I've frozen the account with the bank and I'll wait to hear from you. We don't have anything that needs to be paid right away and we have a new Treasurer beginning January one."

"Sounds good judge. I should be able to get back in touch with you right after the new-year. "

"Thanks Fred."

****

That night after the 4-12 PM roll call, Rheault found Tommasi in the supervisor's office.

"Fredso, what's up?"

"Do you have a few minutes?"

"Yea, I'm on the desk for the first half of the night, then Mugsy will be in for the second half." Mike McGuire was the other sergeant assigned to the 4-12 shift. He got the nickname one night at a police choir practice which stuck throughout his career.

After Fred brought the Sergeant up to speed on what Judge Marshall told him, Tommasi sat in thought for a few moments.

"What we'll need to get are Anderson's bank records. You probably have enough to arrest him now with what Judge Marshall told you and what I'm seeing here, but if we see deposits for the same amount in his personal account or his business accounts, that's just icing on the cake. I'd guess his business accounts since it would be easier to launder the money."

"Yea, I agree," Fred said. I'll start working on the search warrants right after New Year's."

"That'll be good. By the way, are you and the bride doing anything for New Years?" Tommasi asked.

"Naw, that's just amateur night, we're staying home and we'll watch the ball drop on TV. How about you."

"I'm working until midnight and my wife said she'd wait up for me and we'll have a quick new year's drink when I get home."

Authors note: When cops get together after work and have a few drinks, it's known as choir practice. The bottles are referred to as choir books, and of course, the cops who are drinking, are called choir boys. It is believed that this practice was started in LA and was made popular by Joseph Wambaugh's 1975 book, The Choir Boys.

****

Chapter 2
January-February 1995

Rheault was able to determine which bank Anderson had his accounts by the cancelled checks. By Friday January 7th, he had the warrants drawn out for both Anderson's personal and business accounts and presented them to the manager of the bank with the admonishment that if he told Anderson or anyone about the search warrants, he would be an accessory. The warrants were signed by a judge other than Bob Marshall because of a conflict of interest. Rheault also asked for the individual deposit slips since the Kiwanis checks could be one of many check deposits on any given day. Rheault had the paperwork by Sunday January 9th and he and Tommasi went over them that night.

As it turned out, Anderson had deposited most of the checks directly into his business account, separate from deposit slips that were from the business. He then took some of the cash out, and redeposited the cash in both his personal account and business accounts.

One of the checks from the Kiwanis was mad out to a Pam McEvoy for $1000 from the college scholarship fund. When Rheault showed this to Judge Marshall, the judge stated that there was no Pam McEvoy on the scholarship list.

Rheault then went to the bank where it was cashed and the manager was able to pull a video of when the deposit was made. The video showed Robert Anderson, and a girl later identified as Pam McEvoy, cashing the check. The video also showed Anderson pocketing the money while in the bank.

****

"Hmm, I wonder who does his book keeping." Tommasi said.

"I already found out," answered Fred. "My sister works with his mother-in-law at the cleaners. The mother-in-law lives with Anderson and his wife and I went in one day last week and just began talking about the business. His mother-in-law told me an old family friend who studied accounting in college does the bookkeeping. She does it part-time for him."

"So we probably don't want to talk to her before we arrest him. If she's a family friend, she'll probably tip him off," Tommasi said.

"I agree, but after we arrest him we'll talk to her and if necessary, subpoena her to a grand jury," Rheault answered.

"Good plan."

Rheault obtained an arrest Warrant for Anderson the next day and then called judge Marshall.

****

January 10, 1994

Fred Rheault was once again shown into Judge Marshall's chambers and after he was seated told him about what he and Tommasi did.

"We have everything to arrest Anderson judge, we just need you're okay."

Judge Marshall said nothing. He sat in his seat and was obviously deep in thought.

"Fred, we're not going to go through with the arrest. If we arrest Bob, it'll make the papers, and people will lose faith in the Kiwanis. This will hurt donations."

"Are you going to just let him get away with it judge?"

"No. I'm going to approach him and tell him that he's going to resign from the Kiwanis and then I'm going to tell him he's going to pay us back."

"What happens if he just denies everything or just refuses to pay back the money?"

"I don't think that will happen Fred, but if it does, I'll cross that bridge then. In the meantime, both you and Tommasi did a great job and I'll be letting Chief Ross know."

Fred was quiet for a few moments before saying anything. "No problem judge. If you have a change of heart, let me know."

"Once again, thanks Fred."

When confronted, Anderson denied everything.

****

After the 4 PM roll call, Fred walked into the supervisor's office where Tommasi was organizing paperwork.

"You're not going to believe this."

"Let me guess, Judge Marshall decided not to go forward with the Anderson arrest."

"Yea, how'd you know?"

"I'm not surprised. When I was in detectives before making Sergeant, I had a couple of cases involving embezzlement at banks. Once I proved who did it, the banks chose not to press charges. They said that it would be bad for business and they just fired the employee. I figured that would be the same stance from the Kiwanis. Let me guess again, the Judge said it would be 'bad for donations and their public image.'"

"Yea he did."

"I don't agree with that, it just reinforces future bad behavior and stealing. But I'm certainly not going to second guess Bob Marshall," Tommasi said.

"Me neither. He's too good of a guy and judge."

Just then Chief Ross walked into the office.

"I'm glad I got you two guys together. I got a call earlier from Bob Marshall saying what a good job you two did. Nice work."

"Thanks Chief. Aren't you a Kiwanis too?" Fred asked."

"Yea I am, and I don't necessarily disagree with the judge."

Rheault and Tommasi just nodded their heads.

As Rheault was leaving the supervisor's office he turned to Tommasi as an afterthought.

"Hey Tomas, how do porcupines mate?"

"I give up, how do porcupines mate?"

"Very carefully."

"That sounds like a really old joke."
"Yea, but a goodie."

****

At about the same time that Chief Ross was talking to Rheault and Tommasi, Robert Anderson was walking into the Lopez house in Methuen Mass. His business did well this time of year. Not only did he have his weekly clients, but he also had the additional remediation business from frozen pipes that burst and left most homes with extensive water damage as a result. Business was especially good this winter because of the unusually cold weather New England was experiencing. So much for global warming.

After he rang the bell, the door was answered by an absolutely stunning dark haired Hispanic girl.

"Hi, are you Mrs. Lopez? I'm Bob Anderson from ServiceMaster. You called concerning water damage."

"Hi, I'm Francesca Lopez. I think my mom was the one that called you. My Dad's here too. Please come in and I'll get them."

Anderson wiped his feet and then put paper coverings over his shoes so he wouldn't track in dirt. He followed Francesca into the living room and liked everything about her, the way she walked, the way she talked and her very sexy tall figure. While he was appreciating Francesca, her parents came into the living room where introductions and pleasantries were exchanged. They showed Anderson the damage and he noticed it wasn't that bad. Francesca's father told him that they were home when the pipe burst two days ago, and they were able to turn off the water to minimize the damage. Since then, they had cleaned up some of the water and a plumber had replaced the burst pipe.

Anderson told the Lopez's that the cleanup would be no problem and that their homeowners insurance would cover the cleanup less the deductible. He also told them he would take pictures of the damage and send them to the insurance company. Ordinarily, Anderson would have scheduled the cleanup in a couple of days from the time he viewed the damage, but he wanted to see Francesca as soon as possible.

While talking with the family, he learned that both Lopez's worked and Francesca would be home from college in the early afternoon the following day. This was perfect. Anderson would be able to talk to her when her parents weren't there. He made plans to be there with his crew the following day at 1 PM.

****

Anderson was at the Lopez's promptly at one the next day with a crew of two. The crew came in a work van while he arrived in his own car. He showed his crew where the damage was in the finished basement of the split entry house, and while they worked, he spoke to Francesca in the living room. He told her that it shouldn't take more than two to three hours for the clean-up and they should be done right around the time her parents would be home. He found speaking to Francesca was easy and he learned that she worked part-time and she was taking business courses at a local community college, also part time. For Anderson, this was perfect.

"Francesca, how would you like to work for me as a marketing specialist? It would be only a couple of days a week and it would be good experience that would complement your business degree."

"That sounds interesting, what would I have to do and how much would I make?"

"Well, as a marketing specialist, you would accompany me to see new clients, you'll see what I do, and eventually get the hang of it. And while you're training, you'll get paid at ten dollars per hour, and I can work your schedule around school and your other job."

Francesca thought that was really good money and it was more than what she was making now. She told Anderson she liked the idea.

"Listen, I can give you a taste of the job now if you'd like and you'd be getting paid for it. I'm going to leave my crew here to finish up cleaning while I go and talk to a prospective client in Londonderry, NH. Why don't you come, and afterwards, I'll bring you back home."

"Alright, I'll go."

"Great, but before you go, you need to put on something sexy, like a short skirt. Part of the job involves looking sexy and a mini-skirt and heels is a definite plus."

Francesca looked at him for a minute thinking this was a strange request, but then she said she'd be right back after she changed.

When she came back wearing heels and a black mini-skirt, Anderson thought that she was definitely what he wanted.

****

On the way to the house in Londonderry, Anderson explained to her that a woman dressed in a provocative manner can divert a client's attention and win business.

"I'd like you to sit in a very provocative manner," Anderson said. "I'd like you to hike up your skirt and cross your legs. After a while, uncross your legs and sit with your legs open, and when you bend down, show a lot of leg and if some of your ass peaks through, that's good too. You're a very beautiful woman and I think you'll be great for business. Can you do that?"

"I guess so."

****

Francesca pushed Anderson away, slammed the car door, and ran into her house out of breath.

"Sweetheart what happened?" her mother asked.

"That bastard that we hired to clean the house, he offered me a job as a marketing specialist and told me to dress sexy because that gets business, and he was real creepy and suggestive. He was like that all the way up to the house we went to in Londonderry and all the way back. When he pulled into the driveway he started grabbing my boobs while lifting my skirt up and also started grabbing my ass while trying to kiss me. I slapped him, told him to stop, and ran out of the car."

When Francesca's father got home, his wife told him the story. He was wild with anger and she had all she could do to calm him down. However, all agreed that they should report this to the police and went directly to the Methuen Police Station.

At the police station, they met Detective William Rayno and Francesca told him the entire story.

Rayno started an active case and called Salem, NH PD that night.

****

Bill Rayno was a thirty four year veteran of the Methuen Police Department who was working an overtime shift. He was also a Korean War veteran who had lied about his age to enlist in order to serve his country. He had been a Methuen Police Officer since 1960 and was a detective for the past fifteen years. He also served as the department's prosecutor and taught Criminal Justice courses part-time at Northern Essex Community College.

After Rayno had his morning coffee, he called detective Phillips of Salem, NH police department. He had worked a couple of cases with George and they worked well together.

"Detectives, Phillips speaking."

"George, it's Bill Rayno from Methuen."

"How are you doing and what can I do for you?"

"We got a complaint of a sexual assault last night that happened here in Methuen and the guy was from your town. After I took the report, I called your PD and spoke to the Sergeant on the desk, John Tommasi, I teach with him at NECCO."

"Who's the guy?" Phillips asked.

"Tommasi told me that it was someone you know real well, Bob Anderson."

"That cocksucker! Did Tommasi tell you I arrested him back in '84 for assaulting a cheerleader when he was the Athletic Director at the High School?"

"Yea he did, and Tommasi used roughly the same terminology you just used. He also said he wasn't surprised since the best judge of future behavior is past behavior."

"Yea, the girl he assaulted passed a polygraph and there was no doubt in my mind he was guilty. He got off in court up in Hampton because of a change in venue. He had the School Superintendent and High School Principle as character witnesses and an old boyfriend of the girl testified that she was always trying to make him jealous. The only good thing that came out of this was he ended up leaving the school and he lost a job he was applying to as the Principal at Merrimac, New Hampshire high school."

"Yea, it seems that the leopard doesn't change his spots," Rayno answered and then continued. "I just wanted to let you know. I'm going to call him at his business and see if he'll come down to the station to be interviewed."

"Let me know what happens, and Bill, will the papers know?"

"Oh yea, the Captain will eventually put out a press release."

"Outstanding. Let me know what happens."

"I will."

It didn't take long for Anderson's imminent arrest to circulate through the Salem Police Department.

Authors note: NECCO is the acronym used for Northern Essex Community College located in Haverhill, Ma.

****

That morning Mary Lucas was in the office with Anderson when she answered the phone.

"Hello. This is Detective Rayno of Methuen PD. Is Robert Anderson there please?"

"Yes, one minute please."

Mary then placed the call on hold and turned towards Anderson. "Robert, it's a detective Rayno from Methuen PD. What's up?"

Anderson was momentarily taken aback before answering.

"I have no idea. I'll take it in my office."

Anderson walked into his office and closed the door.

"Robert Anderson, may I help you?"

Bill wasted no time and got right to the point. "Mr. Anderson, this is Detective Rayno of the Methuen Police. The reason I'm calling is that I took a report from a Francesca Lopez last night that she was sexually assaulted by you in your car. If possible, I'd like you to come down to the police station, I have some questions to ask you. If not, I can come to see you at your home, but I figured you wouldn't want a marked cruiser in your driveway."

Anderson began to sweat. "I don't know what you're talking about. I offered her a job and she came with me to a client, but because of school she didn't want the job."

"Well, that's not the story she told me. Will you be able to come down to the police station here in Methuen?"

Anderson continued to sweat and was thinking what to do. "Yea, I'll be right down there, but what she's saying is a lie because I had another employee with me in my car and she'll say that nothing happened because nothing happened."

Rayno considered this for a moment.

"Alright, you can come down here and write a statement, and then I'll call this employee. Who is it please?"

Anderson wasn't sure who he would use and said, "I'll tell you when I get there," and then hung up.

Rayno doubted that there was another person in the car.

****

After he hung up, Anderson called Linda Stevens who worked for him and lived in South Lawrence. Linda was middle aged and had worked for Anderson for 5 years.

"Hello Linda, this is Robert."

"How are you doing Robert?"

"Not too well. Listen Linda, I just got a call from Methuen Police, a girl that I offered a job to last night said that I sexually assaulted her in my car in her driveway and that couldn't be further from the truth."

Anderson then went on to tell Stevens how he had offered Lopez a job and described her and what she was wearing. He then told her they went to the client's house and then back to her home where he dropped her off.

"When this girl left the car Linda, she asked for more money and when I said no, she slammed the door of the car and said no to the job. I need you to say that you were in the car and I never assaulted her."

"Robert, I can't say that, it's not the truth."

"Listen Linda, I panicked. This cop probably knows how I was accused of assault ten years ago and this will hurt my position. I swear I never touched her and this could jeopardize my marriage, please Linda.

Stevens felt that she was backed in a corner. Okay, I will, but I still think that you should tell the truth. "

"Thanks Linda, I won't forget this."

****

When Anderson walked into the Methuen Police Station, he was escorted into an interview room by the desk Sergeant. Within a few moments, he was joined by detective Rayno who introduced himself and they shook hands. Rayno was also joined by Detective Lieutenant William Simone. Rayno felt that he clearly had the home court advantage. Once again, Rayno wasted no time and wanted to catch Anderson off balance.

"So Robert, you're saying you didn't sexually assault Ms. Lopez and you say you have a witness?"

"Yes I do."

"Please tell us your version of what happened and who is this witness?"

"The witness is one of my employees, Linda Stevens."

Anderson then told both detectives how he offered her a job and how she came on to him with the way she dressed and acted.

"Why do you think she made up this story Mr. Anderson, especially with a witness?" Simone asked

"I think it would be obvious Lieutenant. She was miffed that I wouldn't give her more money and this was her way of getting back at me."

Rayno thought to himself that Anderson was a smug and arrogant bastard.

Simone had expected an answer like this from Anderson and had an immediate follow-up question.

"Is this what that cheerleader thought almost ten years ago to date?"

Anderson lost his cool and yelled, "I was cleared of that and she was trying to make her boyfriend jealous."

"Yes, I'm sure," was all Simone said.

After a pause Rayno said, "Mr. Anderson, would you like to write us a statement as to what happened."

"I certainly would, and just ask Linda Stevens. She'll tell you that little bitch made this up."

"Thank you."

****

After Anderson wrote his statement, he went back to the office and Mary Lucas was still there.

"What was that all about Bob?"

Anderson was confident that nothing would come of this because Stevens would go to bat for him and didn't want his wife to find out. Relations with her were already strained because of his ongoing relationship with Pam McEvoy whom he still said was nothing but platonic.

"It was a misunderstanding Mary, they mistook my car for another car that was believed to be involved in a shooting. You know how violent Lawrence and parts of Methuen are."

"Oh, okay. Glad it's nothing big."

****

The next morning at 10 AM, the desk Sergeant escorted Linda Stevens into the interview room that Anderson was in the day before.

After five minutes, Lt. Simone and Bill Rayno came into the room and introduced themselves. They had decided to take a different tack with Stevens since they strongly suspected that Anderson was lying.

"Ms. Stevens, can we get you a coffee or glass of water," Rayno asked.

"No thank you I'm fine."

"Alright, we'll be recording this interview."

"Ms. Stevens, were you in the car with Robert Anderson and Francesca Lopez the afternoon of Tuesday, January 11."

"Y-yes I was," she said after a brief hesitation.

Both detectives noticed that Stevens sat in the interview chair with her arms around her. This was a defensive position of a witness which was an indication of possible deception.

"Can you please tell us what happened?" Rayno asked.

"Well nothing really."

"Nothing really?" Rayno asked questionably. "Can you be more specific? For instance, where were you sitting in the car, who was in the car and where did you go?"

"Okay, well," Stevens said hesitatingly, "The new girl, Francesca was in the front seat and Robert was just making small talk on the way to a new client's house in Londonderry. He was driving."

"What was the client's name?"

"I'm sorry I don't remember."

"I'm sorry Ms. Stevens, can you speak up please." Both Simone and Rayno could see that she was not comfortable.

"I said I don't remember."

"Did Mr. Anderson tell Francesca to act sexy and show her how to cross her legs, sit, and bend down?"

"If he did, I didn't hear it."

"What happened when you got into the house?"

"Well, Francesca and Robert went into the house and I stayed in the car."

"You stayed in the car?" Simone asked.

"Yes."

"Ms. Stevens, if you stayed in the car, why were you there at all?"

"I guess I'm not sure."

"You're not sure," Rayno asked while pushing away from the table."

"Well, I guess he wanted me to come in originally but decided to let the new girl try things on her own."

"How long were they in the house Ms. Stevens?"

"I'm not really sure, maybe about 10-15 minutes."

"And then what happened?"

"Robert and the new girl came out and we drove back to her house and she got out."

Both Simone and Rayno just sat in their chairs. Bill took some notes and they glanced briefly at each other. They had expected Steven's answers and they had already determined what they would do. Rayno was a very fatherly figure whereas Simone could be more intimidating at over six feet and two-hundred pounds. Simone played the bad cop.

"Ms. Stevens, are you aware that Robert Anderson is being charged with sexual assault."

"I wasn't sure," Stevens said in a soft voice.

"And if he's arrested and found guilty, that means that you lied to us and could be charged as an accessory after the fact. Is that what you want?" Simone said.

Stevens said nothing but looked down while still hugging herself. She then began to rock back and forth. It was at this point that Rayno spoke up in a soft voice.

"Linda, we realize that this is tough for you. We know he's your boss and that puts you in a very difficult position," Rayno then paused for effect.

"If you were to tell us the truth, and signed a statement that you weren't in the car, we wouldn't charge you with anything. As a matter of fact, we would try to leave you out of this."

Stevens looked up at Rayno and he continued in a soft fatherly voice.

"Linda, were you in the car?"

"No I wasn't."

"Did Robert Anderson ask you to lie for him?"

"Yes he did."

"When did he do this?" Rayno asked

"The day that you called him. As a matter of fact, right after you called him."

"And what did he want you to do and what did he say."

"He said that the girl accused him of touching her and that he didn't do it. He also said it would look bad for him because the same thing happened to him back in '84 and he was worried about his marriage. So he just wanted me to say I was in the car and tell you that nothing happened."

"And you were never in the car."

"That's right."

Thank you Linda. We'll write this up and have you sign it. Thank you for your help and you won't be charged with anything.

"Thank you."

****

After Stevens signed the statement, Simone and Rayno met in Simone's office.

"That Anderson is certainly a dirt bag," Simone said.

"Yea he is. I'll get on the paperwork and bring it before the court."

"Nice job Bill. We should be calling you father Rayno," Simone said.

"Bless you my son," Rayno said while laughing. "Confession is good for the soul."

****

When she got home, Linda Stevens made a phone call she was dreading.

"Hello Robert, it's Linda."

"Hi Linda, how'd it go today and thank you for doing that."

"I couldn't lie Robert. They told me I could be arrested too. I told them that I wasn't in the car. Please don't be angry with me."

Anderson said nothing and just hung up.

After he hung up he called his lawyer.

****

A closed door clerk-magistrate hearing was held February 7th in Lawrence District Court and a complaint and summons to court was issued for Robert Anderson for sexual assault and witness tampering on February 10th.

Anderson was served the evening of February 11th at his home by Bill Rayno, with George Phillips and a marked Salem cruiser. Anderson had not told his wife about the incident. Unlike the 1984 incident, Amy was not standing by her man and went through the roof.

Authors note: In Massachusetts, a Clerk Magistrate's Hearing is also known as a "show cause hearing." The evidence is presented by the police prosecutor and the Clerk Magistrate's primary role is to determine whether probable cause exists to require the accused to answer to a criminal charge for a misdemeanor in District Court.

****

Amy and Bob had a terrible verbal argument that evening after the kids went to bed. If there was one good thing that could be said about him, he wasn't physically abusive. For the first time, it was believed by investigators that Amy talked about getting a divorce. This was something Anderson dreaded since not only would he have to split all his money, he would probably have to pay child support and she would most likely get the house and much of his business. He thought of this as he slept on the couch that night. It was also the night he decided he would not let that happen.

Over the next two weeks, Robert Anderson tried to smooth over relations with his wife. However, by the end of February, she told him that she was still considering a divorce.

Authors note: The above was surmised by interviews with investigators.

****

January 24, 1994

Rebecca O'Brien was very happy with the job ServiceMaster had done after they did the clean-up and remediation from a broken pipe that happened a few days previously. She and her husband had moved back into the house that morning after the cleaners left. They put their clothes away and Rebecca noticed that her husband left his gun, a 9mm Smith and Wesson, on the top of his bureau. She was going to put it in his top drawer when the doorbell rang. The owner of the ServiceMaster franchise, Robert Anderson, was at the door. He had called earlier and stated that he wanted to check the work to make sure it was completed to everyone's satisfaction. As she showed him into the bedroom, her phone rang which was in the kitchen. About 10 minutes later, Anderson came out of the bedroom just as she hung up the phone.

Rebecca found him very accommodating. Anderson stated that he had taken pictures of the bedroom before and after the remediation, and would send them to the insurance company and answer any questions they may have.

When her husband came home that night, she mentioned the gun on the bureau. He immediately went into the bedroom to put it away, but couldn't find it. They checked the entire house and still couldn't find it. The following day, after checking the entire house and garage, they reported the theft of the gun to Manchester Police. They had all the guns paperwork and the police entered it into NCIC.

Authors note: NCIC stands for the National Crime Information Center. The NCIC database was created in 1967 under FBI director J. Edgar Hoover. The purpose of the system was to create a centralized information system to facilitate information flow between the numerous law enforcement branches.

February 12, 1994

Detective Roger Beaudet was working on a fraud case when he got a call from dispatch at 9 AM reference a burglary at 11 Manor Parkway. Manor Parkway was an industrial park off of exit 2 on route 93 in Salem. The business at that location had water damage from a burst pipe and the clean-up crew was reporting the theft of three pieces of industrial equipment.

When Beaudet arrived at the scene he spoke to the responding officer and the owners of the equipment, Dan Choate and his partner Robert Meckel who told Beaudet that an industrial fan, heater and dehumidifier, worth about $2000, were stolen sometime during the night. It appeared entry was gained by jimmying the back door.

Beaudet dusted for prints and didn't get anything useable. He then checked adjoining businesses for outside security cameras and found there were none. He did learn that the business next door had a security guard on at night.

Later that night, Beaudet went back to the business and spoke to the security guard who told him that the only thing he noticed was what he thought was a ServiceMaster van, but wasn't sure.

Beaudet did some research and found out that Robert Anderson had a ServiceMaster franchise. He went to Anderson's business the next day unannounced and found Anderson to be very accommodating. Anderson allowed Beaudet to search not only a storage area connected to his business on Raymond Drive in Salem, but all his vans. He found nothing out of the ordinary.

Later that day after checking with other police departments, Beaudet learned that there were no similar thefts. He had the necessary paperwork from the equipment owners and entered it into NCIC.

Beaudet was unaware of the storage area that Anderson had rented on South Policy Street one mile from his business.

****

Chapter 3
Murder Outside the Back Door

Friday, February 25, 1994
11:00 AM

Judith Smith was the manager of Shawmut bank and sitting in her office at the Essex Street branch when her secretary came in her office.

"Mrs. Smith, it's Robert Anderson from ServiceMaster on line one."

Anderson's ServiceMaster franchise had done some initial cleanup from a burst water pipe earlier in the week and there were still dehumidifiers and heaters running in the basement where the damage occurred.

"Oh thank you Maryann, put him through please.

"Hi Judith, it's Bob Anderson from ServiceMaster."

"Hi Bob what's up?"

"Do you remember that dust problem we talked about earlier this week when I was doing the initial cleanup in the basement from the water pipe?"

"Yes I do."

"Well I'm pretty sure it's being caused by the boiler next door in Cherry and Webbs."

"Really?"

"Yea. Both your buildings are old and there are heating and cooling ducts that are connected. Cherry and Webb closed two years ago, and the boiler probably hasn't been serviced. I'd like to come down and take a look at it and I'll need the key to get in."

"Alright, when will you be here?"

"I should be there right after lunch around one."

"That's fine. Ask for Paul Midola. He's the facilities director and besides me, he also has a key to Cherry and Webb. I have a meeting then."

"Sounds good, thanks Judy and I'll be by sometime tomorrow to collect the fans and heaters from the basement and finish the cleanup."

"Thank you Bob."

Author's note: Cherry and Webb, a national chain, closed its Lawrence store in 1992 and after they vacated the premise, the building was eventually repossessed by the Shawmut Bank. The entire 112 year old corporate business declared bankruptcy in 2000, and liquidated all assets to pay off its creditors.

****

When Anderson got to the Shawmut Bank, Paul Midola was waiting for him inside the lobby. He noticed that Anderson had a tool bag with him.

"Hi Mr. Anderson, Mrs. Smith told me to expect you."

"Please call me Bob, and did she tell you we're going to look at the boiler room in the Cherry and Webb building?"

"Yes she did."

"Let's go then."

Both men walked from the back door of the Shawmut bank, which was also used by customers, to a shared parking lot and in the back door.

"The boiler room is downstairs in the basement Bob."

The building still had electricity and as they walked through the building, Midola was familiar with the layout and turned lights on as they want. After going down a long corridor they turned right and he opened a door.

"Here it is."

"Thanks Paul I have to check some stuff, it should take me about ten minutes."

"That's okay, I have some things I have to do anyway. Give a holler when you're ready."

"Thanks."

With that, Anderson entered the boiler room after turning on the light that was inside the door. He closed the door firmly behind him.

He noticed that there were high ceilings, about twelve feet to a dropped ceiling with older tiles that had a brown tint from age. He looked around and opened a closet door. There was a step ladder in there. After a few moments of thought, he concluded that this would be perfect. He spent a few more minutes in the room, exited and called out to Paul Midola. Paul was around the corner and as he walked toward Anderson he asked, "Did you find the problem?"

"Yes I did. Let's go in and tell Judith."

Both Midola and Anderson went back into the bank and told the manager of the problem and scheduled an appointment to deal with it. Anderson then rolled his eyes and clicked his fingers.

"What's the matter Bob?"

"I left one of my tools in the boiler room."

"Okay, Gary can open the door for you," Judith said.

"No need. It's freezing out, why don't you give me the key, I'll get the tool and bring the key back to you in the bank."

"Alright, here it is."

"Thanks."

With that Anderson took the key from Midola, walked over to the Cherry and Webb building and let himself in. He walked into the building waited a few minutes, and then walked directly back to his van and left.

Paul Midola was then approached by one of the tellers who asked him if he could clean up a spill. He forgot all about the key that was never returned to him by Anderson.

****

Bob and Amy Anderson were getting their two daughters ready to go out for dinner. They were going to meet their good friends, Ray Corliss and his wife, Julie, at T-Bones restaurant on route 28, in Salem, NH, one of the favorite spots of their kids. They met the Corliss' there and said hello to a number of friends who also frequented the establishment. T-Bones was one of those spots where everyone knew your name.

For all intents and purposes, the Andersons appeared as the happiest of couples. Robert was a well-respected businessman and held an officers position in the Kiwanis organization. No One knew that he had resigned from the Kiwanis. Both Andersons were close to the Corliss' since the early 80's and the relationship never wavered through Robert's 1984 arrest and subsequent trial.

Corliss left the school district in 1984 and worked in the business world for the past ten years, however, he was once again appointed as Principal of Salem High School and was scheduled to start that summer.

It was a fun dinner and no one noticed anything out of the ordinary. As usual, the children were well-behaved and happy.

On their way home, Julie turned to Ray and said, "Did you notice anything different about Robert and Amy tonight."

"No, not at all. Why?"

"I don't know, just a feeling something was wrong between them."

"I doubt it. They have a good marriage."

On their way home. Amy was quiet as it was believed she was seriously considering divorcing Robert. Unlike in 1984 where she was sure that Robert never assaulted that cheerleader, she was not so sure about the sexual assault charge against him from Francesca Lopez. In addition, she also wondered about his relationship with his new employee, Pam McEvoy, in spite of his assertions that it was a platonic and innocent relationship.

Robert's thoughts were believed to be much darker.

****

Saturday, February 26, 1994
6:54 PM

"Lawrence Police, Dispatcher Torres, you are being recorded."

"Yes. Essex Street bank, Shawmut bank in Lawrence, please, on Essex Street."

"What's the matter?"

"We were here cleaning the bank and we went outside. My wife ..."

""Sir, I can't understand you, you need to slow down."

"It looks like someone beat up my wife."

"They beat up your wife?"

"Yes, hurry up please."

"Seven hundred Essex Street?"

"Essex Street, I don't know, whatever the number is. We're in the back parking lot."

"Are you at the bank by Demoulas?"

"No, right on Essex Street, right in downtown Lawrence."

"Okay, we'll be sending someone."

"The Shawmut bank. Send an ambulance too."

"The Shawmut bank."

"Yes, the Shawmut."

"And that's right downtown."

"Yes."

"Okay."

"Hurry up please."

"Okay, hang on sir while I send police and an ambulance."

After a short pause the dispatcher came back on the phone. "What's your name sir, and where are you?"

"Bob, Bob Anderson and I'm calling from inside the bank. Please hurry."

"We're right around the corner sir. They'll be there shortly."

"Hurry."

Authors note: The police department is located at 90 Lowell Street and the Fire department across the street at 65 Lowell Street, two blocks away from the bank. The Shawmut Bank is located at 305 Essex Street.

****

Sixty Minutes Earlier

Amy Anderson was at home putting her jacket on.

"Don't worry mom, I'll stay warm. Bob wants me to come with him to help clean and I should be back home by 8 o'clock."

It was a cold night and just starting to snow lightly. The Anderson's arrived at Shawmut bank shortly before 6:30 PM where Robert's two other employees, Tracy Enzo and William Prince were waiting for them. They were there to finish the basement cleanup from the burst water pipe.

After hellos were exchanged, Anderson opened the rear door to the Shawmut Bank while Tracy and Bill brought in the cleaning supplies along with Amy.

Once they went in, Robert said, "Bill, why don't you and Tracy go downstairs and start. Whatever you do, don't use the doors to the stairwell, the doors are locked and the alarm will go off if they are even shook. I found that out the hard way once. Amy, would you mind going out getting us some coffee, drinks and snacks?"

"Oh that's okay, we shouldn't be here long" Tracy said.

"Well you never know, besides it's Saturday night. Amy, I'll walk you to the van."

"You don't have to walk me to the van, it's just outside the back door."

"No, it's Lawrence and it's a violent city, I'll walk you."

"Alright suit yourself."

After Bill and Tracy went down, Anderson hit the up button to the elevator and when the doors opened he went in and flipped a switch.

"What did you just do?" Amy asked.

"I just flipped the stop button on the elevator, this way I don't have to wait for it when I come back."

Amy didn't really see the need for it and just shrugged her shoulders.

****

Bill was working in the back room, steam cleaning the carpet while Tracy was working out in the hallway. Bill told Tracy that he forgot something upstairs and pushed the elevator button which didn't light up. He kept on trying with no luck.

"Hey Robert, are you up there?"

"What's the matter?" Tracy asked.

"Elevators not working."

"You can try the stairs."

"We can't do that, it's alarmed, remember?"

"Oh yea, you'll just have to wait for Robert to come back."

"I guess so."

About ten to fifteen minutes later, they heard the elevator coming down.

Prince met him at the elevator and said, "The elevator wasn't working."

Anderson just shrugged his shoulders and said, "I don't know what to tell you, it worked fine for me. I also brought down the mold killer."

"Thanks," Prince said. "I forgot it upstairs and that's why I was trying the elevator."

"Hey Robert, is that a blood spot on your sweatshirt?" Tracy asked.

Anderson froze and looked at his sweatshirt.

"I don't think so."

"He covered it with his hand and went into the bathroom.

"What do you think that was?" Prince asked Tracy.

"I'm not sure. Maybe he and Amy were fooling around and she got carried away," Tracy said.

Prince just smiled and went back to work as Anderson came out of the bathroom.

"That wasn't blood Tracy, just a stain I must have splashed on me while moving the mop bucket. Why don't we leave Bill downstairs to finish up and you and I will start cleaning upstairs."

Tracy nodded her head and said Okay.

With that, they grabbed some supplies and went upstairs via the elevator.

****

About 15 minutes after starting work upstairs, Anderson turned to Tracy and said, "I wonder what's keeping Amy. She was just going down the street? I'm going outside to check."

"Alright," Tracy responded.

About five minutes later, Anderson came running back into the bank screaming and telling Tracy to call the police, Amy was beat up in the van. Prince heard screaming upstairs and went up to investigate.

"Robert, I can't get an outside line," Tracy said.

"Never mind I'll do it."

Prince arrived upstairs and asked what happened.

"Amy's outside in the van and Robert said she was beat up," Tracy said.

"I'll go out to see."

As Anderson was dialing the police he said to Prince, "Don't go out there Bill, it's bad."

"What happened," Prince asked.

"Amy got beat up bad."

After Anderson hung up he said, "I'm going back outside to be with Amy."

Prince went out with Anderson, and when he saw Amy, he wished that he hadn't.

****

Patrolman Arthur Waller was having coffee in the snack room at Lawrence PD when he got the call to respond to the rear parking lot of the Shawmut Bank on Essex Street reference an assault. Waller pulled up close to the ServiceMaster van and saw Robert Anderson in the van cradling his wife's head. There was also a large amount of blood.

"Headquarters this is bad. Tell the ambulance to step on it," he radioed.

Detective Brian Burokas was at the station and when he heard Waller's radio transmission he jumped in his unmarked cruiser and went to the scene. He arrived slightly before the ambulance and he noticed that the only footprints in the freshly fallen snow were leading back and forth from the bank and from Waller's cruiser to the van. He didn't realize the significance of this until later.

When the ambulance arrived, the EMT's ran right to Amy in the van. They noticed the incredible amount of blood and that, surprisingly, she was breathing but it was labored.

"Is that the husband?" Burokas asked Waller.

"Yea, he told me that she was going out for coffee when this happened. His name is Bob Anderson."

"Alright, I'll talk to him. Radio the station and tell them to call Captain Mollohan. This is probably going to be a homicide." Michael Mollohan was the Captain in charge of detectives.

Burokas walked over to Anderson and said, "Let the EMT's work on her Mr. Anderson. I'm Detective Burokas. Can you step over here please? I know this is difficult but can you tell me what happened?"

"My crew, Amy and I came here to clean. I asked my wife to go out for coffee and snacks and I walked her out to the van. You know, because Lawrence is so violent and then I went back into the bank. In about 20 minutes, I was wondering where she was so I went out to take a look, and that's when I found her in the van covered with blood."

"Did you see or hear anything?"

"No nothing."

"Where's your crew now and how many."

"There are two, Tracy and Bill and they're in the bank."

There were additional firemen on the team who arrived in a rescue truck. They walked over to the ambulance that was already there and brought out the stretcher and wheeled it over to the ServiceMaster van.

Burokas was looking at his crime scene going to shit but it couldn't be helped. Care for the victim came first. He wanted to ask Anderson more questions, but his wife was being put in the ambulance.

"Listen Detective, I need to go with my wife."

"No problem." Burokas then turned to the EMT's and asked, "Where are you taking her?"

"The General." Lawrence General Hospital was a 5 minute drive by ambulance.

Burokas then turned to Anderson, "They're going to Lawrence General, we'll send someone over later."

"Okay," Anderson answered and then got into the ambulance with his wife.

Something was bothering Burokas when he received a call from dispatch.

"Headquarters to D5," which was Burokas' designation.

"Go ahead," he answered.

"We contacted Captain Mollohan and he advises that Detective McDonald will be enroute."

"Copy that. In the meantime can you send me another cruiser to help secure the scene?"

"Roger that."

****

Jack McDonald was a Viet Nam vet who joined the Lawrence Police Department in 1968. After 12 years in patrol, he was promoted to detective and was the departments lead homicide investigator. He had just finished dinner with his wife and was settling in to his couch to watch the evening news when he received a call from Captain Mollohan.

"Hey Jack, it's Mike."

"How are ya Cap?"

"Good. We have a potential homicide at the Shawmut Bank on Essex Street. One of the cleaning crew and it looks like it was done in the back parking lot. Can you head over there?

"Absolutely. I'll give Laird a call too." Mike Laird was Jack's partner of 10 years.

"Good. Give me a call later and let me know what you guys got."

****

Jack and Mike met at the station, grabbed their gear, got into an unmarked cruiser and proceeded to the scene. Before they left the station, they were told by the shift commander that state police were notified and Detective Norman Zuk would be responding with a team to process the scene. Zuk was the lead homicide investigator for the State Police and was extremely competent. He and McDonald had worked a number of homicides in the past all to successful conclusions. Zuk got on State Police in 1980 and made detective in 1985. He was driven, talented and had investigated close to 100 homicides throughout the Commonwealth prior to Anderson.

When Jack and Mike arrived at the scene, Burokas was there to meet them and brought them up to speed.

"One other thing guys," Burokas said. "The crime scene got pretty contaminated by the medics and the husband tramping around and there was something bothering me and I finally figured it out. Actually two things."

"Wait one, Zuk come on over here," McDonald said. "Go ahead Brian."

"I was the second guy on the scene right after Waller and there was a slight covering of snow on the ground. Dispatch had said that there was an unknown assailant but the only footprints I saw were those leading from Waller's cruiser to the van and back, and footprints that went to the rear door of the bank and back. If there was an unknown assailant, there should've been more footprints, probably coming from the street to the van, but there weren't. Also, when you get to the hospital, take a look at Anderson's jacket, it's covered in blood because he was cradling her head, but there were also some stains that looked like they were impact stains."

"Are you thinking he did it Brian?" Zuk asked.

"I think it's a distinct possibility. Whenever a wife gets murdered, I look at the husband first."

"I'm with you on that," Zuk answered.

"Norm do you and Brian want to stay here at the scene and Mike and I will go to the hospital and then we'll meet afterwards at the station?" McDonald said.

"That's a plan," Zuk answered while Burokas nodded his head.

Burokas never noticed if there were any footprints to the Cherry and Webb building.

****

When Laird and McDonald arrived at the Lawrence General Hospital, they stopped at the reception area and were told that Amy Anderson was in surgery and were then directed to the waiting room where Robert Anderson was with two other family members.

When they arrived there, they introduced themselves to Robert Anderson who in turn introduced the detectives to Amy's mother who lived with them and family friend, Mary Lucas. Both of the woman seemed in shock, Robert, not so much.

"Robert, I know this is difficult, but we need to talk to you and get as much info as possible so we can get the person who did this," McDonald said.

"Okay," Anderson answered.

Laird turned towards Mary Lucas and Amy's mother, "Ladies, can you excuse us please."

"We'll go get a coffee," Mary said.

As soon as the women left the room, Mike Laird walked over to a chair where Anderson's blood soaked jacket was hanging and said, "Robert we're going to need the jacket please, they may be transfer evidence on it from the person who did this."

"Ahh okay," Anderson answered hesitatingly.

"Alright Robert, please tell us what happened."

Anderson began by telling them how Amy went with him to clean the bank and how she always did this because they could spend some time together since he often worked 50-60 hours per week. He then recounted how they met his crew at the bank, and after they got settled, he walked Amy to the van because Lawrence was so violent. He ended by telling him how he was concerned when she hadn't returned and he went out to check on her.

"I couldn't believe it, she was my entire life. If she doesn't make it, I don't know what I'm going to do," Anderson said.

"Okay Robert, we have some concerns and would like to talk to you again after we speak to your crew and mother-in-law. Would you be able to come to the Lawrence Police Station tomorrow morning?" McDonald said.

"Why do I have to come back? What's the problem?"

"No problem Robert, we want to see what your crew has to say and there are always loose ends. We'll probably have some more questions after the scene is processed."

"Alright, earlier in the morning would be best," Anderson said.

"How's 8 AM?" McDonald said.

"I'll be there."

****

McDonald and Laird then went down to the café and interviewed Mary Lucas and Amy's mother separately. They learned that Mary was a long-time friend of the family and the bookkeeper for Anderson's four ServiceMaster franchises. They also learned that he was spending a lot of money in the past three months in addition to her concern that a fair amount of money was coming into the business from a source that she wasn't aware.

The interview with Robert's mother-in-law was a little more revealing. The detectives learned that she was living with Amy and Bob since they moved into their upscale Golden Oaks address several years ago and what else she had to say added to the detective's suspicions.

"How was the marriage between Amy and Robert?" McDonald asked.

"It was pretty good, but since about the middle of January, I would hear them arguing and sometimes yelling a lot. They always did it after the kids went to bed and never when they were around."

"Did you know what it was about?"

"No I didn't, but I overheard the word divorce once. When I asked Amy what it was about she said that she didn't want to talk about it."

"Thank you ma'am, you've been a big help and my prayers are with your daughter."

"Thank you detective," Amy's mother said as she was getting up.

"Oh wait, one more thing please," McDonald said.

"Certainly."

"Did Amy often go with Robert on jobs to help him out and be together?"

"No, not really. I was really surprised earlier this night when he asked her to go. It rarely happened."

Thank you ma'am. You've been a big help."

****

Laird and McDonald met in the nurse's station of the ICU ward. Jack asked one of the nurses who is the doctor operating on Amy and any idea when he would be done.

He was told the doctor was Edward Covey, a prominent area neurosurgeon, and he had just finished and was washing up.

"Would it be possible to see him?" Laird asked.

"Yes, I'll let him know you are out here."

In a few minutes a tall man wearing blue scrubs walked towards the two Lawrence Detectives."

"Hello Detectives, I'm Doctor Covey, I operated on Mrs. Anderson."

"Both detectives introduced themselves.

"Is she going to make it Doc?" McDonald asked.

"I'm amazed she's still alive. The wounds she has are just not survivable. She has a real will to live, but it's only a matter of time."

"Is there any chance of her becoming conscious?"

"None whatsoever. This was a brutal attack that showed a lot of rage."

"A lot of rage?"

"Oh yes. Three different weapons were used on her."

"She was hit on the head with a blunt instrument four or five times, she was stabbed four times, by the way it wasn't by a knife, it was something that had a blunt point, like a screwdriver, and finally, her neck was slashed with a very sharp object, and that wasn't by a knife either."

"What do you mean?" Laird asked.

"Something very sharp and thin, I would say an instrument similar to a scalpel."

Both detectives processed this.

"Thanks Doc. If there's anything else you think of please call us," McDonald said and then both detectives handed the doctor their business cards.

"I have to go talk to the family now," Covey said.

"One other thing Doc, can you not tell the family, or anyone else for that matter, what you told us on how she was killed. We don't want it to hit the press."

"Of course."

The Detectives then got back into the car and headed back to the station to speak to Trooper Zuk and Detective Burokas.

****

Back at the station, McDonald brought Burokas and Zuk up to speed on what Dr. Covey told them and their conversations with Anderson and the mother-in-law and friend.

"I agree with the Doctor. That shows a tremendous amount of rage in the manner she was killed," Zuk said.

"What really got to me, was how this murderer used three different weapons. You don't see that every day," Laird said."

Zuk then began to bring Laird and McDonald up to date on what happened after they left.

"We ended up impounding the van and we're bringing it to the State Police Lab in Salem. I'm going to personally deliver Anderson's jacket to the lab tomorrow so we can maintain a good chain of custody. What was really interesting was the stories we got from his two workers, Tracy Enzo and William Prince. Both of us interviewed each one separately and they told almost identical stories."

Zuk summed up the interviews and relayed to Laird and McDonald the following:

Both Enzo and Prince were surprised when Anderson asked them what they wanted for snacks and coffee since they weren't going to be at the bank for a long time. In addition, there were snack, soda and coffee vending machines in the basement. Anderson also told them not to use the stairs because it would set off the alarms and the doors were locked. After they went downstairs and Anderson walked his wife to the van, the elevator wouldn't work, and suddenly, it worked when he came back about 15 minutes later, and Tracy Enzo noticed a blood stain on his sweatshirt. He went to the bathroom to wash it off and told her it was just a water stain.

"Huh, let's add to that his mother-in-law said he and his wife had been arguing for the past month," McDonald said.

"The sonofabitch did it," Zuk said after a moment's thought."

Chapter 4
The Investigation

Sunday, February 27

Amy Anderson died at 6:30 AM Sunday morning. Both Lawrence Police and Robert Anderson were notified by the hospital.

****

Robert Anderson arrived at the station promptly at 8 AM with his brother-in-law, Amy's sister's husband, who was a lawyer.

Jack McDonald had just gotten off the phone with Captain Mollohan and came down to meet Anderson after he was notified by dispatch. Anderson introduced him to his brother-in-law and told him he was a lawyer.

"While he be joining us?" McDonald asked.

"No he's here for support and I don't need a lawyer."

"In that case follow me please Robert."

Jack led him into an interview room where Norman Zuk was waiting. McDonald told them that a lawyer accompanied Anderson but is out in the lobby.

"He's Robert's brother-in-law he said he doesn't need him."

Zuk thought that was pretty arrogant which appeared to match Anderson's demeanor.

McDonald and Zuk were seated at an interview table while Mike Laird was in an adjacent room observing via a two way mirror.

When Anderson sat down, he leaned backed and crossed his leg with one arm over the chair. Zuk thought to himself that even his body language was not only arrogant, but not indicative of someone who was in mourning. McDonald started off the interview.

"Robert we're going to read you your Miranda rights and ask you to sign them," McDonald said. "You're not under arrest but this is just a formality we do in any interview of this nature."

McDonald then read and explained the rights to Anderson which he signed. He asked Anderson his first question.

"Robert, can you please recount the events of last night up to the point when you accompanied your wife to the hospital in the ambulance.

"We left the house at about six and arrived at the Shawmut bank at around six-thirty. Tracy and Billy were waiting for us. I let everyone in and I told Billy and Tracy to go downstairs and finish the clean-up that we started earlier in the week. I then asked my wife to go get us snacks. I told her I'd walk her out to the van since there's, you know, so much violence in Lawrence." At this point Anderson appeared to choke up and all three detectives felt it was forced.

"I walked her to the van and then came back in the bank and went downstairs to join my crew."

"Robert let me interrupt you for a moment," McDonald said and then continued.

"Did you tell your crew not to use the stairs because it was alarmed?"

"Ahh, yes, I guess I did. The maintenance guy told me something about that earlier in the week."

"After you went down to the basement with your crew and wife, you came back up in the elevator?"

"Yes."

After a pause McDonald continued, "Did you know that Bill Prince tried to use the elevator to get back up but it wasn't working?"

Anderson paused for a few seconds before answering. "Ahh yea, when I came back, I noticed the doors were still open, I must have unknowingly flipped the stop switch. That's not uncommon that I do that when it's after hours and I'm cleaning a place."

"So then what happened?"

"I walked her out to the van and came back in."

"Did you look around to see if there was anyone in the area?"

"No I didn't."

"Then what did you do?"

"I went back in and helped my crew and after about twenty minutes I was wondering what was keeping Amy. That's when I went back out." At this point, Anderson choked up and suppressed a sob. McDonald thought it was worthy of an Oscar nomination.

The detectives said nothing for a few minutes and then Zuk spoke up.

"Mr. Anderson, when you joined your crew in the basement, Ms. Enzo said that she noticed a blood stain on your sweatshirt."

Anderson began to shake his head. "I told her it was a splash from the mop bucket."

"Just to be sure, we'd like to bring that sweatshirt to the state lab."

"No problem detective Zuk, but it's already been through the wash."

This time McDonald shook his head and then said, "Robert, one of the things Detective Burokas noticed when he arrived was there were footprints in the fresh snow leading from the van to the rear door of the bank and then back again and that was all. If your wife was killed as a result of city violence there would have been footprints from the road. There were none. Let me be blunt Robert, everything is pointing at you. So how do you explain that Robert?"

"Very simple, I don't. This interview is over and you detectives need to do your job. I don't believe this. My wife was the most important thing in my life and I'm leaving to go bury her."

"I'll walk you out Robert," McDonald said.

As Jack McDonald walked Anderson to the front door of the police station, nothing was said, and nothing would be said until later in the week.

****

When McDonald went back to the interview room, Laird joined them from the observation room.

"What do you think guys?" McDonald asked.

"I think there's very little doubt, he did it," Laird said. All three nodded their heads

"We need to find the murder weapons," McDonald said and then continued, "Right before Anderson got here I was on the phone with Mollohan and he authorized all the overtime we need today to try and find the murder weapons."

"They could be anywhere," Laird said.

"Yea, some guys are going to be dumpster diving," McDonald said.

"Not only that, but sewers, trash-cans and maybe even the canals. We can't rule out the fact that he may have had an accomplice, like in the Charles Stuart murder case. If so, we should probably get some State Police Divers and check the canals tomorrow if we don't find anything today," Zuk said.

"Shit that's right. If I remember correctly, Stuart's brother was the accomplice," Laird said.

"Yea and he dumped the gun and her pocketbook off a bridge in Revere," Zuk answered.

"It's going to be cold for the divers," McDonald said.

"It won't be too bad," Zuk said, "They have dry suits and thick thermal underwear underneath. One of the guys told me that they're good for about two hours before getting cold. They also have full face masks and Sherwood regulators that don't freeze up in this weather."

"Alright, let's do this today; Norman why don't you handle what's happening at the state lab and coordinate the dive team for tomorrow if we come up with nothing today, and Mike and I will organize the search for the weapons," McDonald said.

Zuk then said, "I'm also going to do some research on Anderson. I want to see if he has a brother. I know the head of detectives in Salem, NH, Dick Dunn and I'll give him a call. I want to see what they have on Anderson."

"Sounds like a plan. Let's meet back here at four and see what we have."

Author's note: Dumpster diving is police slang for searching through trash cans and dumpsters for evidence of a crime.

****

"Hey Tony, how are you doing in there?" a laughing Jack McDonald yelled.

Tony Lorenzo had been in detectives for 10 years and he was one of the six lucky dumpster divers that were split into two teams of three. There was also a team of four firemen that were wearing exposure suits and checking the sewers. His team was currently searching the dumpster behind the Shawmut bank. It was a dirty job and the cold February weather made it even worse. He popped his head out of the dumpster and Jack saw that he was wearing one of the fire department hazardous waste suits and a face mask with attached filter. His team had been at it for three hours.

"Everyone's a comedian," Lorenzo responded as he popped his head out and waded through the garbage. "No luck so far Jack, this cold weather is both good and bad. It keeps the smell down from the food that was thrown away but I'm also freezing my ass off. How are the other teams doing?"

"Laird is with the other team and they're doing about as well as you guys. They're currently checking trash-cans. I haven't checked to see how the fire department is doing in the sewers."

Lorenzo smiled to himself as he had a thought.

"Hey Jack, what would you call it if one of the firemen died while checking the sewers?"

"I don't know, what?"
"Sewer-side."
"Everyone's a comedian," McDonald answered.

****

Norman Zuk was at the state lab in Salem, Ma. And was talking to the blood splatter expert, Morgan Dexter.

Dexter had her Master's degree in Biochemistry and had been working at the state lab for five years. She was considered to be highly capable and knowledgeable.

"So what you're telling me is that some of the blood on Anderson's jacket was a result of impact splatters?" Zuk asked.

"Yes. It's called a projected impacted stain. If you hit someone hard enough and penetrate the skin, or the skull as in this case, blood will splatter back onto the individual," Dexter then showed Zuk the splatter stains on the jacket.

"As you can see, the splatter stains are circular in nature with a tail at the end. No doubt about it, the person who was wearing this jacket hit someone forcefully with a heavy object."

"Thanks Morgan, much appreciated."

"One other thing detective, there's some white residue on the jacket too. After it gets analyzed, I'll let you know the results."

"Thanks again."

****

There were a lot of people working overtime at the State Lab on Sunday because of the murder. The next person that Zuk spoke to was David Coe, a chemist for the State Lab.

"Hi Dave, what do you have?"

"I'll be doing a DNA analysis of the blood on Anderson's jacket and also on the murder weapons if and when you get them. It'll take around three days to get results. I already did a blood analysis and the blood on Anderson's jacket is the same type as Amy's. Probably no doubt it's hers, but we'll need the DNA for court."

"When we find the weapons, you'll be the first to know," Zuk said.

Zuk next called Dr. Leonard Atkins who was one of the state's medical examiners who had responded to the crime scene the previous night.

"Hi Doc it's Norman."

"Hi Norm. What can I do for you?"

"I just want to confirm when the autopsy is. Are you still planning on doing it tomorrow? I'd like to be there."

"Yea I was. How's 2 PM sound?"

"That works. And it'll be at the Tewksbury State Hospital?" Zuk asked.

"That's correct."

"See you then."

Zuk next went to an office that Police used at the State Lab and called Salem, NH PD on the landline. He identified himself and asked for Lieutenant Dunn. The dispatcher advised him that he wasn't in. Zuk left his cell phone number and asked the dispatcher if he could call the Lieutenant and have him return his call.

Fifteen minutes later, Dick Dunn called him.

"Norman how are you?"

"Busy Dick. We had a murder of a woman from your town. An Amy Anderson and the evidence is pointing to her husband Robert. He seems like a real low-life." Zuk then told the Lieutenant the circumstances of the murder from the previous night and Anderson's interview that morning.

"Rest assured Norman. We know him and by calling him a low-life we're giving all low-life's of the world a bad name."

Dunn then told Zuk about Anderson's assault charge and trial of 1984 and the recent sexual assault charge out of Methuen and his embezzling from the Kiwanis.

"He certainly is of low character. Can I come up there and get copies of everything?"

"Sure, Fred Rheault is the on call detective and he worked the Kiwanis case. He's familiar with everything else."

"Thanks Dick, much appreciated."

****

Fred Rheault met Norman at the front door of Salem, PD and introduced himself.

"My lieutenant told me that you're investigating the murder of Amy Anderson and you think it was her husband?"

"Yea, everything is pointing towards him."

"It wouldn't surprise me. I just finished an embezzlement case against him where he took 5K from the Kiwanis when he was treasurer, and I have copies of that report and a 1984 sexual assault case that he beat in court. Incidentally, his wife stood beside him in 1984. The girl he assaulted was a cheerleader and Amy said to the papers that girl put him and the family through hell."

"Thanks. Lt. Dunn also told me he has a pending sexual assault case out of Methuen."

"Yea, Bill Rayno is handling it. I think he's scheduled for court this week too."

"That's interesting. I'll call Bill tomorrow. He's a good man. Anderson's mother-in-law told me at the hospital that he and Amy had been arguing lately. She didn't know what it was about, I guess it could be that assault," Zuk said.

"Could be. Back in eighty-four when he was arrested, they were both teachers at the high school. From what my younger sisters tell me, everyone loved Amy as a person and a teacher, him, not so much. They described him as creepy. He ended up leaving the school and teaching later that year and started his cleaning business."

"Do you know if he has any siblings?"

"I think he may have a brother. Let me check with dispatch."

After Rheault spoke with dispatch and they ran a check, he turned to Zuk."

"It looks like he has a brother who lives here in town. His mother is still alive and living in Florida. His brother's name is Harold, and outside of some minor traffic violations, he has no record."

"Do you think we could go see him? I'm working with Jack McDonald and Mike Laird in Lawrence and we were wondering if Anderson might have had an accomplice. We were comparing the case to the Stuart murder in Boston and Stuart's accomplice was his brother."

"That's interesting. Yea, lets jump in my unmarked and we'll go visit him."

****

It was 2 PM when Rheault and Zuk introduced themselves to Harold Anderson and showed their ID's.

After Harold invited them in he showed them to the living room and asked, "What's this all about?"

"Mr. Anderson, I take it you're aware of your sister-in-laws murder?" Zuk answered.

"Yes I am, my brother called this morning, but why are you here?"

"We're trying to be as complete as possible. Were you aware of any recent conflict between your brother and Amy?"

"You're not blaming Robert for the murder are you? They had a great marriage."

"We have no suspects at the time and we're just crossing the t's and dotting the i's. Amy's mom stated that for the past month they had been arguing a lot which was unusual," Zuk said.

"No I'm not aware of any problems, and I resent the fact that you're looking at my brother in that way."

"I understand Mr. Anderson but we would be remiss if we didn't follow up. Where were you Friday night sir?"

"Great, now you're looking at me. My wife and I got a babysitter and we went to the 99's about 5 PM in Salem for dinner, stayed there until about seven and came back home. It was starting to snow."

"Thank you sir, and I suspect that there were people there you know."

"Of course."

"One more question. Can you think of anyone who might want to do harm against your sister-in-law?"

"No I can't. But Robert told me that this was a result of all that violence in Lawrence. Are you looking at that?"

"Yes sir we are. Well if there's anything you can think of, regardless of how remote, please contact Detective Rheault or myself. Here's my card."

****

After both detectives left, Harold called his brother.

"Hey Bob, it's Harry. I just got visited by two cops. A Trooper Zuk from Mass State Police and Rheault from Salem. It seemed like they're trying to blame Amy's murder on you."

"Yea I know. Zuk interviewed me this morning along with two Lawrence detectives and I walked out on them."

"Listen, I know this is tough, if there's anything I can do, call me."

"Thanks Harry, much appreciated."

****

"Well that went pretty much as expected," Rheault said once they got in the car.

"Yea I'm not surprised. We can pretty much cancel him out as an accomplice since there's plenty of people who can substantiate his alibi. Still, he may know something."

"Yea possible. Listen Norm I'm in all week if there's anything you need, call."

"Will do and thanks Fred."

****

After leaving Salem PD, Zuk met McDonald and Laird at Lawrence PD and brought them up to date on what transpired at the state lab and his interview with Anderson's brother.

"The blood splatter stains may be enough to arrest him, but not nearly enough for a conviction." Both Lawrence detectives nodded their heads in agreement

"Did you guys have any luck on the murder weapons?"

"Goose eggs, we came up with nothing," Laird answered.

"Okay, I'll notify the dive team. They probably won't start until late morning."

"I don't envy them diving in the Lawrence canals," McDonald said. "Let's meet here tomorrow at 9 and go from there."

"See you then."

****

Chapter 5
The Investigation

Monday, February 28

There was a meeting the next morning in detectives that was run by Captain Mollohan. Trooper Zuk and Lieutenant Jim Milone of the state police were also there. Prior to the meeting Zuk had called Detective Bill Rayno of Methuen and told those present at the meeting about the sexual assault charge pending against Anderson. Court was scheduled for later that week but it was anticipated that it would be postponed because of the murder.

It was agreed that there would be three teams of two detectives each that would canvas the neighborhood around the Shawmut bank. Milone and Zuk would provide support for the dive team and Zuk would go to Tewksbury hospital for the autopsy, and they would all meet again that night to compare notes.

The State Police dive team did find a rusted gun in a canal that was probably linked to a previous shooting, but it had evidently been in the canal for a number of years. They found nothing related to the murder.

Lawrence detectives, literally went from door to door in the business district of Essex and Common Streets. Most of the buildings were between three and four stories with businesses on the ground floor and apartments on the upper levels. It was tedious work and yielded no results.

****

Zuk walked into the Tewksbury State Hospital thirty minutes early and after identifying himself at the front desk was directed to where the autopsy of Amy Anderson was to take place. Dr Leonard Atkins was already there and he began the autopsy as soon as Zuk put his mask on and a smock in the event of any splatter. As Dr Atkins performed the autopsy, he started his cassette and began recording his findings. When he finished, he turned off the tape and turned to Zuk.

"Norman, whoever did this had a lot of rage. It was a brutal beating. She was bludgeoned four or five times, stabbed with something that had a blunt point and then cut with a very sharp object. It's truly amazing she lived until the next morning. I totally agree with Dr. Covey who performed the surgery, these wounds were not survivable."

"Thanks Doc. You said pretty much the same thing that Dr. Covey said. Let me know when you have the toxicology report."

"I will Norm, it should be by the end of the week, and one other thing, there were no defensive wounds, so whoever did this, she knew, or never saw it coming."

"Thanks again Doc."

****

That evening, the Lawrence detectives met with Norman Zuk and Lieutenant Milone and assistant Essex County District Attorney Fred McAlary. The day's investigations turned up very little. McDonald said the detectives even checked the roofs with no luck. Unless something turned up overnight, tomorrow would be more of the same. They agreed to meet at 9 AM the following morning.

Before they broke, Zuk informed everyone as to what Dr. Atkins told him about the possibility that Amy knew the assailant since there were no defensive wounds.

Jack McDonald thought to himself that it's looking more and more like her husband did it. Now, if they could only find the murder weapons.

****

That night, the headline in the Eagle Tribune read, "Teacher-Mom is Murdered." Assistant District Attorney Fred McAlary stated to the paper that they had no suspects and an arrest is not imminent. Chief Joseph St Germain acted as the spokesman for Lawrence PD. He confirmed what McAlary said in addition to stating that there appeared to be nothing stolen from Amy. He also told reporters that Robert Anderson was the last person to see Amy alive and the murder weapons had not been found. St Germain stated that Amy Anderson died as a result of the wounds she sustained during the attack with no mention of the brutality of the attack.

In another article, reporter Bill Murphy interviewed the superintendent of Salem schools Henry LaBranche in addition to a number of teachers at Salem high and the school principal, Robert DeSimone.

Murphy reported that she was an extremely popular teacher who had graduated from Salem High in 1970 and was also Miss Salem High her senior year. She attended Plymouth State College and met her husband Robert when they were both student teaching at Salem High in 1975. They both received full time teaching positions at Salem High and were married two years later. Amy was also a mother of an eight and ten year old daughter at the time of her death.

    Amy taught English at Salem High for twenty years and was loved by her students and other teachers. She was always there for her students and was very nurturing towards new teachers. One teacher stated that, "the kids absolutely worshipped her."

    Over the years she served as a class advisor, an advisor to the Key Club and assisted with the schools mentor program.

    In Amy's obituary, the wake was going to be held on Tuesday and Wednesday from 3-5 in the afternoon and 7-9 at night at the Douglas and Johnson funeral home and the funeral would be Thursday at St. Joseph Church with a burial at the Pine Grove Cemetery in Salem.

****

    That evening, there was a get together at Robert and Amy Anderson's home for family and friends. It was extremely crowded, and when Bill Prince dropped by, he didn't want to impose and only stayed a short time.

****

Chapter 6
The Investigation
The Murder Weapons

Tuesday, March 1

Judith Smith was deep in thought when she walked into her office early Tuesday morning at Shawmut bank. She had been contacted Sunday about the murder of Amy Anderson and the search for the murder weapons. She read the previous night in the Eagle Tribune the police had no suspects and hadn't found the murder weapons. She also heard a rumor that the police were considering Robert Anderson as a suspect. Just then her facilities director, Paul Midola, walked by her office.

"Paul can you come in here a moment please."

"Sure what's up?"

"Did you ever get the key back from Robert Anderson when he went back into Cherry and Webbs?"

"Come to think of it, no I didn't."

"Alright, I'll call him later and ask for it," Smith said. "Sorry about that, I forgot."

"Don't bother, I'll take care of it, thanks."

After a few moments thought, she called Lawrence PD and asked for the detective who was handling the Anderson murder."

****

Jack was on his second cup of coffee and people were filing into detectives for the morning meeting when his phone rang.

"Detective McDonald," he answered.

"Hi Detective, this is Judith Smith, the manager of Shawmut bank."

"Yes Mrs. Smith, what can I do for you?"

"Well I read in the paper how you haven't found the murder weapons and there's a rumor going around that you suspect Robert Anderson."

"I can confirm that we haven't found the murder weapons, but I won't comment on the case."

"I understand, but I was wondering if you'd like to know that my facilities director had given the key to the vacant Cherry and Webb building to Robert Anderson the day before the murder, but never got it back."

"Yes I am interested in that. Would you happen to have another key?"

"Yes I would."

"Thank you. Let me get a team together and we'll be there within an hour."

****

Jack arrived at the Shawmut bank forty minutes later with his partner Mike Laird, Mark Rivit, another Lawrence detective and Trooper Zuk. They were shown into Judith Smith's office where she relayed to them the story of how Robert Anderson told her that there was a dust problem and how he believed it originated in the adjoining Cherry and Webb building.

"My facilities director, Paul Midola, went with him and after they left the building, Robert said he forgot something and went back into the building after Paul gave him the key. Paul said he never got the key back from Robert."

"Is Paul around?" Jack asked.

"Yes, let me call him in."

When Paul entered the room, introductions were made.

"Did you accompany Anderson into the building?" Jack asked.

"Yes I did. He went right into the boiler room and was there for about ten minutes."

"Were you with him all the time?"

"No I wasn't. I was in another room down the hall and around the corner, and he called out to me when he was done."

"Do you think he left the room and went anywhere else?"

"I don't know but the door to the boiler room is big and heavy and it squeaks when you open and close it. I may have heard him if he left."

After a moment's thought, McDonald turned towards Judith, "Would you mind if we had a look?"

"Not at all detective, I'll have Paul go with you and show you the way around."

"Thanks Judith, much appreciated."

The detectives followed Midola to the rear of the Cherry and Webb building where he opened the back door, turned on the lights and showed them where the boiler room was in the basement. Zuk noticed how loud the door squeaked when opened. The room was rectangular with high ceilings and was about twenty by thirty feet with a tiled floor. It was filled with duct work and some shelves. The detectives each took a wall and began their search.

About ten minutes into the search McDonald noticed a stain on the floor.

"Hey guys, take a look at this," as he pointed to the stained floor.

"What does this look like to you?"

Zuk bent down and took a look at the round shaped blobs on the floor. It was reddish-brown in color.

"It looks like dried blood splatters," Zuk said.

"With that, all four detectives looked up.

"Will you look at that, one of the ceiling tiles is askew," Zuk said.

"Do you think somethings hid up there?" Rivit said.

"I'll bet a dollars to a pennies there's something hid up there," Laird said and with that he started walking towards the wall he was previously searching. "There's a closet with a ladder in it over here. Before touching the ladder, Laird put on a pair of gloves and brought it to where the one ceiling tile was raised.

He had a small flashlight with him and he went up the ladder.

"It looks like I may have another blood stain on the ceiling tile. It looks like it may be a smear." He then moved the tile and peered inside with his flash light. He then let out a long slow whistle.

"We have our murder weapons guys. I got a big adjustable wrench, a phillips screwdriver and it looks like a carpet cutter and a pair of gloves all covered with blood and probably pieces of flesh and dark brown hair. They're in a trash bag. Holy shit, wait a minute, I got two guns up here too. It looks like a small caliber automatic and a 9 mm."

"Alright, leave everything as is Mike. Let's secure the area and I'll call the state crime lab," Zuk said as he started to dial his cell phone.

Before exiting the building, they searched the entire building to ascertain that no one else was in the building. Mark Rivit stayed outside the boiler room while McDonald and Laird called for two cruisers to stand guard outside the building until the lab techs arrived.

"Even though we don't need it, I'm going to get a search warrant for the building," Zuk said.

"Never hurts to err on the safe side," McDonald replied.

"I'll head back to the station to do the warrant, I have my laptop with me."

****

The lab techs arrived shortly after Zuk finished the search warrant and had it signed by a judge from the district court next to the station.

Four hours later, the techs were done.

Zuk went up to the tech supervisor.

"What do you think?"

"I think we have the murder weapons and more," David Caine answered. "It also looks that we may have a print or two on the guns. The DNA evidence won't be ready until later this week, but we'll have the prints by tonight along with basic blood info. I've already got the okay to work overtime."

"Much appreciated Dave. Call me anytime tonight."

"Will do."

Zuk then brought his boss, Lieutenant Milone up to date. Jack McDonald and Mike Laird did the same with their bosses and Chief St. Germain.

****

That evenings Eagle Tribune ran a front page article on how Robert Anderson was facing a sexual assault charge out of Methuen, Ma. The article stated that he was scheduled to appear in Lawrence District Court the following day but it was cancelled as a result of his wife's murder and rescheduled for March 17th. Bill Rayno from Methuen PD gave a general description of the charges against Anderson and his actions that led up to the department charging Anderson, including an employee he asked to lie for him by saying she was in the van where the assault occurred, and attest that it never happened.

The article also related how Anderson was found innocent of a similar charge in 1984 of simple assault on a cheerleader and went into the facts of the case on how he lifted the cheerleader's skirt.

In a separate article that night, the Tribune reported how friends, colleagues and students were dealing with death of the popular teacher.

John Lawton, a psychology teacher who had taught at Salem High for thirty years had Amy in class when she was a student. Amy was a student, friend and colleague to him. He stated that, "She was a beautiful person both inside and out. She was loaded with energy and was loved by all of us."

Another colleague, Cathy Snow, who taught at Salem for eighteen years said, "When I had a bad day, I always felt better after talking with her. No matter what was happening in Amy's life, she made the best of it and put a smile on her face."

Several students were moved to write poems about her, one of them being Jennifer Moran. The final stanza of the 17 year-old sophomore's poem read:

No words could sum up her life, her tragically untimely demise
For her eyes were often afire, and her smile a quiet sunrise
I will always remember the world she showed me, unexplored
This doves brilliant flight, and the fact that
The pen is really mightier than the sword
"In loving memory, Mrs. Amy Anderson."

****

It was a cold night with wind chills below ten degrees but this didn't stop the line to Amy Anderson's wake being out the door, down the driveway and onto the sidewalk in front of the Douglas and Johnson funeral home located on Main Street in Salem, NH. Susan Smith and her husband Don were two of the people who were in that line and braving the freezing temperatures. After forty-five minutes in line, they finally made it into the door and were talking to Robert Anderson.

"Robert we're so sorry," Susan said.

"Thanks, but can you believe what the papers are saying about me? That's all bullshit. There's all this random violence in Lawrence and they write that about me."

Susan was at a loss for words. She didn't expect that from a grieving husband and mumbled not to worry about it.

As she and Don were walking back to the car, Don said, "He didn't seem very sad did he?"

"That's because the sonofabitch did it," Susan answered.

Don just nodded his head.

****

Zuk's phone rang at 9:15 that night.

"Hi Norm, it's Dave."

"Hi Dave, what's up?"

"We got two prints off the guns. One's a partial from the 9 mm, and it looks like its Anderson. On the .25-caliber, we got a full print and it is definitely Anderson's. In addition, the blood on the wrench, screw driver and carpet cutter is the same type as Amy Andersons, but we won't know definitely until we get the DNA results, probably by Friday."

"That's great news, thanks. I'll drop by the lab tomorrow morning first thing.

"See you then."

After hanging up, Norman then called Jack McDonald on his cell phone.

"Jack, it's Norm, one of the prints on the small caliber gun comes back to Anderson.

"Great news, we got the sonofabitch."

"Absolutely. I'll be by tomorrow morning after I drop by the state lab to get the results and then we can bang out an arrest warrant."

"See you then."

****

Chapter 7
The Investigation
Wednesday March 2

The Arrest

It was 9:30 in the morning by the time Norman Zuk and Lieutenant Milone arrived at Lawrence, PD. Also in detectives were Chief St. Germain and Captain Mollohan.

"Hi Norman, I already have the arrest warrant written, take a look at it," McDonald said.

Zuk sat at a spare desk he was using and read it over.

"This is good Jack. Between the blood splatters and the fingerprints, this is more than enough. We need to bring Salem PD on board too after the warrant gets signed."

"Definitely, I'll give Captain Gould a call at Salem and let him know what's happening. He's the head of detectives. We then have to decide when and where we're going to arrest Anderson," Captain Mollohan said.

"Yea, there's a wake today from 3-5 in the afternoon and then 7-9 at night. The funeral is at 10 tomorrow morning at a church in Salem," Laird said.

Mollohan nodded his head. "Let's do this. Jack go to court and get the warrant signed and try to keep it on the QT. I don't want this getting out before we arrest him, especially the papers. I'll call Salem and set up a meeting for early this afternoon and that's where we'll plan the arrest."

****

Captain Gould walked into detectives and closed the door. Lieutenant Dunn was there along with Fred Rheault, Roger Beaudet and George Phillips.

"Well George, you're finally going to be vindicated, Lawrence has an arrest warrant for Robert Anderson for the murder of his wife.

"That bastard," Phillips said.

"They found the murder weapons yesterday along with some guns and they got Anderson's fingerprints off them. There were also some bloody gloves. We have a 1 PM meeting scheduled with them and we're going to decide when and where to get him."

"I'd like to be there," Phillips said.

"That's a given," Gould said. "I have to go tell the Chief.

****

When State Police and Lawrence detectives arrived at Salem PD, the rumor mill was in full force at the station as to whether Bob Anderson was going to be arrested. Prior to the Lawrence detectives going to Salem, Chief St Germain received a phone call from a number of papers concerning the rumors that an arrest on Amy Anderson's murder was imminent. Chief St Germain stated, "The rumors are out of control. There seems to be a new one every five minutes. There are no suspects and no arrests.

****

The meeting started by Jack McDonald and Norman Zuk bringing the Salem detectives on board on what they had for evidence on Anderson and how it was obtained.

"When do you want to arrest him Jack?" Gould asked.

"Norm can best answer that."

"Initially we were thinking that we would arrest him tomorrow after the funeral and mercy meal. But I got a call from one of my snitches that right after the funeral, he and his girlfriend, someone named Pam McEvoy out of North Andover, are heading off to Colorado for a skiing vacation."

"You got to be shitting me?" Rheault said.

"Why am I not surprised," Phillips answered.

"One of the things we should take into consideration is the family. It's going to be tough on them, especially the little girls," Gould said.

Everyone nodded their heads.

"How about tonight after the wake," Rheault suggested, then went on. "We've had a guy out there doing traffic yesterday and we can set up a loose surveillance on Anderson after the wake this afternoon."

"That sounds good Fred. We can also station a cruiser outside their house on Golden Oaks to keep onlookers away. Anyone have anything to add."

I'm good with that. How about you Jim?" Mollohan said.

"That a go," responded Lieutenant Milone."

"Alright, I'll arrange for the cruisers and light surveillance of Anderson and we'll meet back here at 7 PM."

****

That nights Eagle Tribune sported two headlines concerning the Anderson murder. Despite the police efforts to contain information the Tribune had the headline, "Police fend off rumors of imminent teacher murder arrest."

The Tribune reported that there were rumors that someone had confessed to the murder and Chief St. Germain's answer. Brad Goldstein of the Tribune called Chief St. Germain in the afternoon and asked if there was any truth to the rumor that the killer had been caught on bank video bragging about the murder. Chief St. Germain neither confirmed or denied the rumor and reiterated that there were no suspects and no arrests. Goldstein, being a seasoned reporter thought this was odd since police like to appease the public and generally say that there a number of "persons of interest" they are looking at. Goldstein thought that an arrest was definitely imminent.

The rumors were so widespread that a New Hampshire TV station was camped out in front of the Lawrence Police Station in the hope of seeing the suspect being marched into the station.

The second headline in the Tribune quoted the Mayor of Lawrence, Mary Claire Kennedy. The headline read, "Mayor: City's image hurt by slaying." At the time, Lawrence was besieged by drugs and the city appeared to be a major hub for the drug trade, stolen cars and associated violence. At the time, Lawrence had amongst the highest violent crime rates in Massachusetts.

The Mayor stated, "It's unfortunate the murder contributed to the negative image that the city has, but I think that anyone following this story realizes this murder could have happened anywhere. It could've happened in Salem, NH, Methuen, North Andover or Andover. It's unfortunate for the city that it happened in Lawrence and I've seen no evidence to suggest this city is any less safe now than before this murder happened."

Chief St. Germain was quoted as saying, "Cases of random violence are uncommon despite the city's reputation for crime. Most crimes are drug related as was the other murder in the city this year."

****

That night at Douglas and Johnson Funeral Home, the crowd was even larger than the night before. Fred Rheault and Jack McDonald sat in an unmarked cruiser in the parking lot.

"This crowd will be here way past nine o'clock," McDonald said.

"Yea, it was like this last night too, we'll have to make a decision when to pop him, I'm going to give Gould a call," Rheault answered.

After Rheault called Gould, the Captain said he would get back to him.

In five minutes, Rheault's cell phone rang.

"Fred, it's Al."

"What's up?"

"We decided that regardless of how crowded it may be, we're going to go in and arrest him at 9:30."

"Alright, but I'll tell you now, the crowd will still be out the door by then."

"Okay, we'll deal with it."

****

At 9:30 two unmarked cruisers and a marked Salem cruiser pulled into the parking lot of the Douglas and Johnson funeral home. As Rheault predicted, the crowd was still out the door. Besides the on duty patrolman, there was Lieutenant Milone and Norman Zuk from Mass State Police, Mike Laird and Captain Mollohan from Lawrence and Detectives Beaudet and Phillips from Salem along with Captain Gould. Before all went in, they were joined by Rheault and McDonald.

As they walked in though the main entrance of the funeral home, all eyes turned towards them. They walked directly to the receiving line where Robert Anderson was standing. Jack McDonald had the arrest warrant and was in the front of the line with George Phillips next to him. Phillips looked Anderson straight in the eyes.

"Robert, time to go to the PD," McDonald said.

"What's this all about?" Anderson asked.

"Look at the casket Robert," McDonald replied.

Anderson was momentarily speechless and then recovered.

"You had to do it now, at the wake? Really? You couldn't wait until after the funeral?"

Detective Phillips continued to look at Anderson directly in the eyes.

"Hey Bob, if it wasn't for you, there wouldn't be a wake and funeral."

****

As Fred Rheault put the handcuffs on Anderson, the crowd stood in stunned silence. Amy's brother, who never warmed to Robert Anderson over the years, lunged at him and had to be restrained. A number of family members started crying.

As Anderson was walked out the door, Ray Corliss, who had been at the wake both nights said to Rheault, "Hey Fred, I hope you know what you're doing."

Fred stopped and turned towards Corliss.

"Hey Ray, when it comes to premeditated first degree murder, I always know what I'm doing," Fred turned and continued to walk Anderson out the funeral home door and into the waiting cruiser.

****

At the station Anderson was booked and fingerprinted. While being fingerprinted, he expressed a concern that some fingerprint ink was getting on his clothes.

Roger Beaudet turned to him and said, "Don't worry Bob, where you're going, that won't be a concern."

Chapter 8
The Investigation
Follow up

Thursday, March 3

Despite a blizzard that hit the New England area the following morning, the funeral for Amy Anderson went as planned at St. Joseph's Church in Salem. It was a tough winter in the Northeast and it was their fifteenth storm of the season with flooding expected in the coastal area. Up to two feet of snow was expected in some areas.

The family of Amy Anderson banded together with some of them believing that it was a case of mistaken identity and Robert was really innocent. Amy's sister, her husband and two children moved into the house at 187 Golden Oaks to help take care of the two girls with their grandmother, and to try to maintain some continuity for them. It was a very close family and they gathered at the house after the funeral and mercy meal.

That morning in Salem District Court, Anderson was represented by Gregory Moffatt, and extradition to Massachusetts was waived. Anderson was then transported by Lawrence Detectives to the Essex County House of Correction located in Middleton, Ma. It is a county maximum security prison that can house over 1200 inmates. He was scheduled to be arraigned the following morning at Lawrence District Court.

****

That morning was also busy for the investigators. Trooper Zuk received a phone call from Dr. Leonard Atkins at the state lab when the funeral was being held.

"Norm, we need something from Amy Anderson in order to get DNA for comparison purposes."

"You've got to be kidding me," Zuk said. She's being buried now. Are you saying we need to get a court order to exhume her after she's buried?"

"No, just some hair will do. Maybe from a hairbrush from her home or bed."

"Alright, I'll contact Rheault at Salem, and have him get a search warrant. We'll call the family ahead of time and we'll see what we can do. Maybe we can get a hairbrush or a pillowcase."

"That would be fine Norm, keep me in the loop."

Zuk then called Rheault and relayed the conversation to him from Dr. Atkins.

"No problem Norm. I'll get to work on the warrant now and call Judge Marshall. I should be done sometime around noon. We're going to have a cruiser at the funeral because of the number of people expected and then probably station one at the house after."

"Alright, I'll be up there sometime around one. This weather certainly sucks, especially for the funeral," Zuk replied.

"Yea, there's never a good day for it. This is especially bad."

Rheault started to work on the search warrant for Amy Anderson's hair. He didn't know it, but it would be one of many that he would do in the next month.

****

Rheault had told Captain Gould what was happening and after the search warrant was completed, walked into Gould's office shortly after noon.

"How do you want to work this? They should just about be going to the mercy meal now and then the family and immediate friends are going back to the house."

After thinking for a minute Gould answered.

"Let's go see Judge Marshall at the mercy meal and see what he wants us to do."

"Alright want to head up now?

"Yea, just you and me Fred, we'll keep it low key."

"I'll get the car and let dispatch know to let Zuk in when he gets here."

****

The mercy meal was being held in town and was very crowded. The detectives were able to locate Judge Marshall and approached him.

"Hi Judge," Captain Gould said. "Sorry to bother you but we got a request from Mass State Police to get some samples of Amy's hair, probably from a hair brush or maybe pillow for DNA purposes."

Judge Marshall just shook his head while looking at the search warrant.

"Let me go speak to Amy's sister. I'll be right back," Judge Marshall said.

In a few minutes the Judge returned.

"I spoke to Amy's sister and her main concern is the girls, so let's try to minimize the impact. Fred you know the family so why don't you go alone into the house, Amy's sister will meet you and she'll show you where everything is. She said sometime between 3-4 PM will be good."

"Absolutely judge and thanks. I also expect I'll probably have another search warrant or two looking for evidence and we'll be sure to notify you and come to you," Rheault answered.

"Fred, how sure are you of his guilt.

Rheault didn't hesitate, "One-hundred percent judge."

"That's what I thought."

As Gould and Rheault were leaving, they went past Ray Corliss. All three just nodded to each other.

****

Rheault and Zuk arrived at the Anderson house at 3:30 and spoke to Wes Decker who was stationed there in a marked cruiser. It was still snowing hard.

Rheault got out of his unmarked car and approached the cruiser.

"How's it going Wes?"

"Not bad, the crowd has thinned out and a couple of reporters showed up but I asked them to leave since the family didn't want to speak to anyone. They were pretty good about it with only a couple snapping pics of the house and that was it. I heard you guys got a search warrant."

"No big deal, just looking for some hair from a brush or something for DNA comparisons."

"Okay, let me know if you need anything. If not, I'm staying in my warm dry cruiser."

"Well you know what they say Wes."

"What's that?"

"A good cop never gets wet or go hungry."

With that, Decker just smiled and began to eat a sandwich he had packed and poured some coffee into a cup from his thermos.

****

Fred was met at the door by Amy's sister and after pleasantries were exchanged and condolences offered, she brought Rheault to the bathroom that Amy used and pointed out some specific items. Rheault was able to remove a curling iron brush, a hair brush, make-up bag, two pillow cases and human hair that was in a waste basket. Rheault "bagged and tagged" the items and gave Amy's sister the receipt from the search warrant. Little was said.

****

Back at the station, they were met by Jack McDonald and Michael Laird.

Zuk had the evidence from the Anderson house and the four detectives had a brief meeting.

"Fred, I think we're going to need you for a couple of more search warrants," Jack McDonald said.

"Let me guess, for the key to Cherry and Webb."

"Yup, that and maybe for gloves and trash bags similar to the ones we found with the murder weapons. We brought you copies of our reports."

"Alright. I'll get started on them first thing in the morning. I'll call Judge Marshall tonight and let him know we're coming and I'll ask him if he wants me to call the family. I know he wants to minimize the impact on the kids. Why don't we meet here about 12:30 tomorrow?"

Everyone nodded and began the struggle home during the storm except for Norman Zuk, who first stopped at the State Lab in Salem, Mass.

****

Earlier that day at 9 AM, a press conference was heled at the Salem, NH police department concerning the arrest of Robert Anderson. Present, amongst others, were Chief James Ross of Salem, Chief St Germaine of Lawrence and Lieutenant John Milone of Mass State Police. A picture of the three were included under the Eagle Tribunes Headline, "Husband Arrested as Killer at Slain Teachers Wake."

Chief St. Germaine did most of the talking and told reporters that an arrest warrant for Anderson was obtained after the murder weapons were found in the Cherry and Webb Building and his fingerprint was found on a gun that was in a plastic trash bag with those weapons. He also stated that Anderson was a suspect right from the beginning and no one bought his story that the murder was a function of random city violence. He also stated that it didn't appear that robbery was a motive since nothing was missing from inside the van or from Amy Anderson's personal belongings.

When the Tribune was published, they stated that many investigators felt that this was a Charles Stuart type murder that had occurred five years previously in Boston and was still relatively fresh in everyone's minds since there was a TV documentary in addition to numerous books written on the subject.

The Tribune also reported that despite Robert Anderson's claim that he and Amy had an idyllic marriage, they recounted his arrest in 1984 for sexual assault of a student and his current charge of sexual assault that had been scheduled for court earlier in the week. They also reported that sources indicated that this had put a strain on the marriage.

While Jim Patton of the Tribune was covering the press conference, reporter Brad Goldstein was interviewing Fred McAlary, the assistant District Attorney for Essex County in Massachusetts who was scheduled to prosecute Anderson. When asked about the motive for the killing, he replied, "There are only two motives for doing anything: money and women."

McAlary also affirmed that this was a similar case to the Charles Stuart murder where the murder of a wife was blamed on random city violence.

****

Weekend, March 4-6

The Lawrence police had started a crime line earlier in the week and when Norman Zuk checked it Friday morning, there were a number of calls that shed some light on Anderson's motive for killing his wife. Specifically, there were two phone calls that told about the affair that Anderson was having with Pam McEvoy and there was one phone call that not only pointed out Anderson's recent arrest for sexual assault, but also mentioned his assault on a high school cheerleader in 1984.

Zuk then researched Pam McEvoy and was able to find her phone number which he subsequently called. McEvoy expressed concern over Anderson's arrest and stated that she wasn't surprised that Anderson killed his wife. She was very cooperative with Zuk and she was not considered an accessory. She mentioned to Zuk that they were planning a ski vacation to Colorado in addition to telling Zuk about a safety deposit box with what she believed held $50,000 in cash.

Zuk relayed this information to Attorney McAlary who was arraigning Anderson that morning in Lawrence District Court.

At 10 AM McAlary appeared before Judge Michael Stella in Lawrence District Court. Anderson was represented by Attorney Moffatt.

At the arraignment, McAlary describe the events of the murder with special emphasis on the violence of the attack. He also mentioned Anderson's two prior sexual assault arrests and the four month affair with Pam McEvoy. He asked for no bail.

Moffett argued that Fergusson had strong ties to the community and the need for his children to have a parent present for his daughters. Moffett professed Anderson's innocence and alleged the killer was still free, quite possibly roaming the streets of Lawrence.

McAlary countered that police had received information that Anderson was planning a skiing vacation in Colorado with the woman he was having an affair, and that he has considerable assets including a safety deposit box with $50,000 in cash which could make him a flight risk. The Eagle Tribune also reported that McAlary once again compared Anderson to the "Notorious wife killer, Charles Stuart."

Judge Stella accepted Anderson's not guilty plea and ordered he be held without bail, but did schedule a bail hearing for Tuesday, March 8.

On his way out of court, Zuk was asked a number of questions by Jim Patton of the tribune. Jim was well respected and his son Shawn, was a patrolman at Salem, NH PD.

Zuk stated to Patton that when he first met Anderson, he felt that Anderson was only mildly upset and not overcome with grief.

Zuk then left court enroute to Salem PD.

****

After Zuk walked into detectives at Salem, he brought everyone on board on the arraignment and then asked Fred how everything was going with the search warrant.

"Pretty good," Rheault answered. I ended up doing two search warrants, one for the home and the other for the business. I then contacted Judge Marshall who called the family and Amy's sister said that she will take the kids out to lunch at a local arcade between 12:30 and 3:30 so we can go then with no effect on the children. I then went to court and Judge Marshall signed both warrants. We're looking for the key to Cherry and Webb and other evidence of the crime, specifically, plastic bags like the one we found the guns and murder weapons in, and gloves similar to the ones we found too."

"That's it, let's go," answered Zuk.

****

The search of the Anderson home at Golden Oaks yielded nothing. However, they hit the jackpot at the ServiceMaster business located at 4 Raymond Ave. They not only found gloves and plastic bags similar to the ones found at Cherry and Webbs, but the commercial fan, heater and humidifier stolen from the Manor Parkway site that was investigated by Roger Beaudet in February. As a result, a subsequent arrest warrant for Robert Anderson was prepared by Rheault and served ex parte.

That nights Eagle Tribune commented on the new evidence found by detectives investigating the murder in addition to giving a synopsis of the murder and arrest of Robert Anderson.

****

Late that afternoon, Jack McDonald was pulled off the Anderson murder and assigned to help Haverhill detectives on a murder investigation where the primary subject, Jose Rivera, lived in Lawrence.

Rivera was arrested the following week for the murder of Tim Campbell, a local businessman, in a case of apparent mistaken identity. Rivera had confused Campbell for a person who had previously engaged with Rivera in a drug deal gone bad. Campbell was shot four times and was reported to have died in agony while pleading for his life. Campbell's girlfriend Paula, who was with him at the time of the murder was also shot. Her injuries were not life threatening and she was subsequently treated and released at the Hale Hospital after a couple of days.

Rivera is believed to be a member of a local gang engaged in drug dealing and stolen cars. He was arrested without incident at a friend's house in Lawrence.

****

On Sunday, March 6, the Tribune's headlines were "Friends ponder Anderson's secret side."

After restating the historical facts of the case, a number of the family's friends and colleagues at school were interviewed by the Tribune and to a person they all thought that they were a happy couple with one person stating that "Robert was not a womanizer." This caused some investigators to nearly choke on their morning coffee.

One person who was interviewed recalled that a grieving Robert Anderson stated to her, "What am I going to do? I lost one of my three musketeers," using his pet name for Amy and the girls.

A friend of the family was in a state of disbelief and still held out hope of his innocence. "It's beyond comprehension. He was a friend of ours. He isn't a violent person. They loved each other. There were never any signs of trouble. Neither one of them ever gave me the impression that something was wrong. In my heart, I just can't believe it."

The very popular principle of the Fisk school, which the daughters attended, was also in a state of disbelief. "Robert was a person who was a lot of fun. If you went to a 60's dance he was there doing the jitterbug, if you went to a cookout, he was there cooking.

The principle also stated that she went to the Anderson home to see the girls and brought them each a stuffed Easter bunny. "I talked to them a long time and asked them what they did over February vacation. They said that they had gone with their mom to the Museum of Fine Arts and out to lunch. I almost died. But it was a wonderful memory for them."

****

Week March 6-11

John Tommasi was working an overtime shift that Monday morning when Fred Rheault came into the supervisor's office.

"Hey Tomas, you're still the Union's president. Do you have Jim Carpenito's cell number?" Jim Carpenito was the Union's lawyer.

"Yea I do. What's up?"

"Well, he's also the lawyer for Amy Anderson's mother who's living with them. I'm going to suggest to him that he tie up Anderson's assets. Some girl that he was seeing was interviewed by Zuk on Friday and said that he has a safety deposit box stashed away with $50,000 in cash and possibly other assets."

Tommasi let out a long whistle. "I'm not surprised."

Rheault returned to his desk after getting the phone number from Tommasi and called Carpenito.

When his phone rang, Jim noticed that it was a Town number and answered it right off.

"Hello Jim, Fred Rheault from the police station."

"Hi Fred, how are you?" Jim knew Fred from a previous grievance he was involved in and also knew he was aware that Fred was one of the primary investigators in the murder of Amy Anderson.

Fred brought Jim up to date on the statements by Pam McEvoy and recommended that he may want to attach Anderson's assets, particularly, the presence of a secret safety deposit box.

After Fred hung up, Carpenito called Amy's mother and suggested to her a course of action. He also proposed that Amy's sister and brother-in-law be there too. He gladly said that he would come to the house after dinner that night.

After meeting with the family, Jim Carpenito stayed up half the night preparing ex parte subpoenas for nine local banks in order to gain access to any records and/or safety deposit boxes that might be in Anderson's name. He had previously contacted the Rockingham County Sheriff's office and Deputy Lt Al D'Urso was assigned to serve the subpoenas the next day. Al was a retired patrolman from Salem PD and was working approximately thirty hours/week for the County Sheriff.

****

That Tuesday morning saw Robert Anderson in Lawrence District Court before Judge Stella for his bail hearing. He was being represented by Gary Crossen. Crossen argued that family members were here in court in support of Anderson and that he should be released on $250,000 bail while stressing that his client is innocent and that the district attorney's office is sensationalizing the case "to preclude any rational consideration of bail" by comparing the crime to the Charles Stuart murder case. He also invoked Anderson's longtime residence in the state and strong connections to the area, particularly with his two young daughters.

Attorney McAlary, for the state, concentrated on the gruesomeness of the murder and the overwhelming evidence pointing to Robert Anderson. McAlary also mentioned the new charges against Anderson for the theft of commercial equipment from a rival firm.

The sitting Judge, Kevin Herily, ruled that Anderson would continue to be held without bail.

****

Jim Carpenito, Fred Rheault and Al D'Urso had a busy day travelling to nine local banks. The search for the safety deposit bank proved fruitful as they located the safety deposit box at a bank different than the one where he and Amy had a joint account. In the box they found a savings book to that bank totaling $54,000, $38,000 in cash in one-hundred dollar bills, and negotiable securities valued at $178,000.

After informing the family, Carpenito went back to his office and began the paperwork for a wrongful death suit against Anderson on behalf of the children and Guardians.

Authors Note: The above information was gleaned through interviews with investigators, court records and articles from the Eagle Tribune and Salem Observer. No information was provided by Attorney Carpenito because of Lawyer/Client privilege.

****

That night's Eagle Tribune's headlines read, "Family stands by wife-slay suspect." The Tribune reported that the lawyer for Robert Anderson, Gary Crossen, said that the family of Robert's slain wife, as well as his own family, are standing by him as he awaits trial. They also reported that Anderson was awaiting trial for sexual assault of an employee at the time of his wife's death, in addition to having been found not guilty of a similar charge in 1984.

****

On Wednesday, Carpenito finished the required court papers and filed at $5 million dollar wrongful death suit against Robert Anderson with the Rockingham County Superior Court. The trial to attach all assets was set for the following May 6 in Superior Court. Amy's family was quickly believing that Anderson was not innocent.

****

On Wednesday morning, Rheault received a call from Judge Marshall.
"Hello Fred, it's Bob Marshall."
"Judge, what can I do for you?"
"Fred I've decided to go forward with a warrant for Robert Anderson for theft by deception. I want to do it only on one specific item."
"No problem Judge. Which item?"
"I have a cancelled check for $1000 that was made out to Pam McEvoy. It was made out to her as a scholarship check and she was supposedly from Salem High. I double checked with the principal's office and

there is no such student. Am I correct in believing that this was his girlfriend?"

"Yes Judge, you're correct. I'll get on this right away."

"Thanks Fred. This really stinks."

"I know judge. I'll be over this afternoon to get it signed."

That afternoon's Tribune featured an article that read, "Anderson still has defenders." Anderson's lawyer once again re-iterated that both sides of the family are still supporting him but did not mention which family members from Amy's side. He also acknowledged that Robert's parents were living in the home at 187 Golden Oaks along with the two girls, Amy's mother, sister and her husband.

According to the Tribune, Assistant District Attorney McAlary stated "Mr. Crossen took a certain amount of liberty saying family members of the victim are supporting Mr. Anderson. I think that a number of family members are still in shock and they are looking out for the best interest of the two girls."

In a separate article, the Tribune reported that Anderson has an outstanding arrest warrant for stealing over $2000 worth of commercial cleaning equipment from a rival, in addition to another arrest warrant for theft by deception for a check written to Pam McEvoy for $1000. Both warrants were felonies.

In addition, the Tribune stated that Anderson was under investigation by the Manchester, NH police department for the theft of a 9 mm handgun which was found with the murder weapons of Amy Anderson.

****

Friday's Tribune ran the headline, "Slain teacher's family sues accused husband." The Tribune reported that the family of Amy Anderson sued Robert for $5 million in a wrongful death lawsuit. At the same time, Amy's mother and sister received custody of the two children while obtaining a restraining order keeping Robert Anderson away from the house in the event he was granted bail. This seemed unlikely since all his assets had been attached, including an attachment on any properties he may own which prevented him from selling it. It was also very doubtful that he would get PR bail.

The Tribune reported that the attachments were prepared by the family's lawyer, James Carpenito, and included: the home at 187 Golden Oaks, and rental properties in Salem, Florida and the mountains plus his four ServiceMaster franchises.

Amy's mother was quoted as saying, "This is the hardest thing I have done in my life, but I must protect the children. Their welfare is the most important thing right now. I have cared for them since the day they were born."

Amy's family also issued a statement expressing hope that Robert Anderson would eventually be found innocent.

At the hearing, Anderson's lawyer, Gary Crossen, continued to say that both sides of the family support his client despite evidence that was presented by prosecutors linking him to the crime. Once again, he didn't mention who supported Robert from Amy's family.

****

Investigation 1994 -1995

On March 22, Amy's sister, who continued to live at 187 Golden Oaks, was cleaning the cupboard above the refrigerator when she noticed a key with blood on it. She immediately called the Salem Police and her call was forwarded to Detective Rheault.

After Rheault went to the home and took the key, he called Norman Zuk and Jack McDonald, and met them at Lawrence PD, where he gave the key to Zuk. Zuk in turn took the key to the State Lab in Salem.

The key turned out to be the missing one from Cherry and Webb with Amy Anderson's blood on it.

****

As a result of Anderson's assets being attached, Attorney Crossen, on March 30, asked to be removed as Anderson's lawyer because of his questionable financial status. Crossen was granted his request by the Essex County Court and Anderson was assigned a public defender who represented him on May 9th at his bail hearing. At this hearing he was denied bail and Lawrence McGuire was eventually assigned as his public defender. The trial was expected to go forward sometime in the fall of 1994.

Anderson's appeal to not have his assets attached as a result of the five million dollar wrongful death suit brought by Amy's family, was also denied by Judge Gray of the Rockingham County Superior Court in New

Hampshire. Anderson's assets were estimated to be in the vicinity of $1.2 million. In 2022 dollars, that would equate to $2.38 million.

****

Lawrence McGuire was a very competent lawyer who eventually went on to private practice in Salem, Ma, however, Robert Anderson was looking for a very high profile lawyer. In July of 1994, Anderson's parents refinanced they house in Florida and with the money from the refinance contracted with Attorney Jay Carney in Boston Ma. At the time, Carney was said to be the best defense lawyer in the Commonwealth.

His representation of Anderson was approved by the court in early August, and upon request of defense counsel, the trial was postponed to 1995 in order to allow Carney time to familiarize himself with the case. This was not unreasonable given the voluminous amount of paperwork that he needed to go through and process.

During late February of 1995, the Salem Observer ran a one year memorial to Amy Anderson and gave a synopsis of the case during the past year. They ended the article by saying a court date had not yet been set.

During the month of March, a court Date of June 5, 1995 was set to be held in the Essex County Superior Court.

****

During August of 1994, Trooper Zuk had occasion to interview William Prince again. During the interview Zuk showed Prince pictures of the murder weapons not really expecting a reaction. However, he was surprised when Prince said that he recognized the phillips screwdriver that was one of the murder weapons.

Prince noticed that the screwdriver had the initials R. A. M. on its shaft and said that they had done remediation work the previous year at a Russell Massahos' house in Salem. He recognized the screwdriver because it was borrowed by Anderson form the owner of the house, Russ Massahos, who owned the R&J Getty station on Main St. in Salem. Russ had previously died and Zuk subsequently interviewed his son, Jim Massahos, who inherited the station. Jim confirmed his dad's ownership of the screwdriver and he was subsequently scheduled to testify at court.

During the same interview of Prince, Bill also stated that Anderson had a storage facility on South Policy Street in Salem. He went on to say that Anderson stored furniture in this unit that he took from homes that the company, ServiceMaster, remediated. Anderson would tell the owners, that the furniture was beyond repair and he would dispose of it for them. Anderson then cleaned the furniture, stored it, and sold it for a profit.

Fred Rheault was once again called upon for a search warrant, which was granted, and the furniture was found and recovered from the storage area on South Policy.

The owners were eventually contacted. Since many of them were able to get insurance money for the furniture, the various insurance companies were then contacted.

Theft by Deception charges were brought against Anderson pending the outcome of the Murder Trial.

****

Chapter 9

The Trial

Sunday, June 4, 1995

The trial of Robert Anderson was set to begin on Monday, June, 5 1995 in the Essex County Superior Court located in Newburyport, Ma. By the time the trial started, he had been in the Essex County Jail in Middleton, Ma for fifteen months. At the time of the trial, Robert was 44 and the trial was expected to last three weeks.

His Defense Attorney was still J W Carney who was being assisted by attorney Andrew D'Angelo. The defense was expected to claim that Robert Anderson did not kill his wife who he was very much in love with, but it was an act of random urban violence that Lawrence Ma was known for.

The prosecuting attorney, Fred McAlary, is expected to show that the marriage was anything but blissful, and will portray Anderson as a man motivated to kill his wife as a result of his love of money and a younger women who totally captivated him. According to the Eagle Tribune, McAlary stated, "He didn't want to share his money which would be caused by a divorce, and he was completely infatuated by a younger girl." He went on to say that the case against Anderson will be built on highly persuasive circumstantial evidence. The bag containing the murder weapons and stolen guns is, in fact, the "smoking gun" that was found in the deserted Cherry and Webb building adjacent to the Shawmut bank. The key to the Cherry and Webb building was given to Robert Anderson the day before, and was eventually found in his house. It is also expected that McAlary will present evidence that the Andersons marriage was very unstable as a result of the January, 1994 sexual assault charge on Anderson out of Methuen, and Amy Anderson's knowledge of Robert's relationship with Pamela McEvoy, who had since moved to Washington, DC after the murder of Amy. The monetary loss would be significant since, in addition to the ServiceMaster franchises, the Andersons owned the home on Golden Oaks, condominiums in New Hampshire and Florida, and a duplex home in Salem, NH that was used for rentals.

By contrast, Carney is expected to portray Anderson as a successful and loving family man who owned several cleaning franchises, and was driven to provide a good life for his wife and family. He did not kill his wife, and the killer is still at large. It is unknown how he will address the matter of Robert Anderson's fingerprints on one of two stolen guns that were found with the murder weapons, and a bloody glove and towels similar to those found in the ServiceMaster van where Amy Anderson was killed.

****

Fred McAlary had been a prosecutor since 1979 after graduating from the University of Connecticut. He had won several high profile murder cases including Irwin Hartford Jr. who had molested and killed a 13 year old boy in Haverhill, Ma in 1993. The case also withstood two appeals.

McAlary was given high accolades by other attorneys. John Gillen of North Andover stated that

McAlary is a seasoned, thorough prosecutor who is skillful at building successful cases. He is not flamboyant, and with his six foot, 190 pound frame he is well spoken and has significant courtroom presence. Mary McCabe, a Lawrence lawyer, stated that McAlary is highly respected and has a likable personality that endears him to judges and juries alike. He is not an obnoxious explosive prosecutor and respects all witnesses.

The Tribune also reported that many local newspapers, especially the Boston papers, continued to compare the Anderson murder case to the Charles Stuart murder of his wife Carol, in Boston, in 1989.

Sixty-five year old Superior Court Judge Robert Barton would preside over the trial. Robert Barton was the son of Russian immigrants. He grew up in Everett, Ma and graduated from Dartmouth College in 1952, and three years later from the Boston University School of Law. He then enlisted in the Marines as an officer candidate and was subsequently stationed in Okinawa. From Okinawa he went to San Francisco where he met his wife Norma, a flight attendant. They eventually settled in Bedford, Ma where he served a number of years as an assistant district attorney in Cambridge. He then went into private practice renting an office from famed defense lawyer, F Lee Bailey.

Barton was appointed to the bench in 1978 by then Governor Michael Dukakis.

****

While jury selection was occurring and both sides were gearing up for the first day in court, so too was the trial of

OJ Simpson for the murder of his ex-wife, Nicole Brown Smith and her friend, Ronald Goldman. The trial began in January of 1995 and would continue until early October when Judge Ito would give final instructions to the jury.

On June 3, Judge Ito ruled that the jury could see more than 40 photos of the autopsy and grisly murder scene.

Simpson had been arraigned in July 1994, more than one month after the murder.

****

June 5, 1995
Monday

The first day of court dealt a victory for the defense. Judge Barton ruled that Robert Anderson's previous arrests, in 1984 and January of 1994, for sexual assault, would not be admissible at trial since it may prejudice the jury. This was a stark blow to the prosecution since McAlary planned showing how this was, in part, why Amy Anderson was upset with Robert and was contemplating a divorce. This would make it more difficult for McAlary detailing the motives Anderson had for killing his wife and continuing an open relationship with Pam McEvoy, while keeping his wealth intact. McAlary wanted to show that while Amy stood behind her husband in the 1984 trial, she wasn't in 1994.

When asked about the ruling by Bill Murphy the Eagle Tribune reporter, Prosecutor McAlary replied, "Everything you lose hurts, however I will still be able to present highly convincing evidence that convicts

Anderson." Methuen prosecutors withdrew the sexual assault charge after Anderson was arrested for the murder of Amy.

At this time, eight jurors were picked and Judge Barton was hoping to pick another eight jurors so opening arguments could be heard the next day. There would be twelve jurors that would decide the case along with four alternates.

During jury selection later that day, Anderson was present with his lawyer and was seen occasionally whispering in his ear. The rest of the jury was picked that day.

****

During the OJ Simpson trial, Judge Ito had previously ruled that the prosecution could introduce evidence of previous spousal abuse when OJ Simpson and Nicole Brown Simpson were married.

****

June 6, 1995
Tuesday

The defense surprised the court and observers by announcing that Robert Anderson would testify on his behalf. "Not only would he testify", said Carney "but he insisted on testifying."

The Tribune reported that Jay Carney stated, "From day one, my client has adamantly denied his guilt and has looked forward to getting his day in court."

Many court observers felt that this was unusual since the defense usually waits until the very end of the trial to announce if the defendant(s) will testify.

However, Carney wasn't through with dropping bombs. He also announced in court that he subpoenaed the Anderson's two children to testify in court. This was opposed by the family and the prosecution.

James Carpenito, who continued to represent Amy's family, stated that he would fight the subpoenas. Prosecutor McAlary stated to Judge Barton that forcing the children to testify could cause them irreparable harm. He also inferred that these could be court room theatrics by the defense.

The testimony of the children was expected to revolve around the fact that they never saw they parents fight or argue, thereby allowing the defense to try and undermine the prosecution's contention that the marriage was in trouble.

Judge Barton indicated that the defense must persuade him the children's testimony would be relevant and significant, and he will decide prior to the defense calling witnesses.

Amy Anderson's sister who was co-guardian of the Anderson girls stated, "Mr. Anderson is a clever con man who deceived his wife and family and others in their hometown into believing he was a loving family man. He was so successful at the deception, he thinks that he can now bamboozle a jury. He's confident, and he thinks he lies so well that he'll be able to get away with it. He had us all duped for many years."

She also went on to say that Robert Anderson and her sister did argue, but never in front of the children. She also stated, surprising some, that Robert was a loving father to the girls, teaching them to ski and taking them on outings. She was disheartened, though, that attorney Carney would even consider having the young children testify.

Some legal experts commented that if the prosecution was to stipulate that Anderson was a loving father, this may preclude the children testifying.

Amy's sister went on to say that she is still living with the children and her mother in her sister's home on Golden Oaks. She and her husband felt that it was hard for them to do it because of the memories, but all family members believed that it would be best for the children to maintain some continuity. It was very much a testament to the love, closeness and devotion of Amy's family.

Amy's sister and mother, the two co-guardians of the children, were expected to be the prosecutions first witnesses.

The motions and proceedings took up most of the morning and after lunch, the jury was expected to tour the murder scene behind Shawmut bank and the deserted Cherry and Webb store where the murder weapons were found. Opening statements were scheduled for the following morning.

****

June 7, 1995
Wednesday

There were over fifty people in the courtroom for the opening statements.

Jay Carney began by saying that Amy Anderson was a remarkable, loving woman and mother whose murder was a tragedy.

Police felt pressure to find the killer because of all the media attention and this was indicative of the violence that permeated Lawrence. Carney stated that, "Police felt their reputation was at stake, and under this pressure there was a 'Rush to Judgement,' and they arrested the wrong man, Robert Anderson. The killer is still out there, and the killer is laughing."

The Defense resumed by trying to plant doubt in the minds of jurors by suggesting another member of the cleaning crew may have killed Amy. Without making an accusation, Carney implied that Bill Prince, the former student Robert Anderson took under his wing, had the opportunity to leave the bank and kill Amy Anderson. Carney stated, "Bob Anderson can tell you where he was when the crew was in the bank. But he didn't know where Billy was the entire time."

Jay Carney next tried to discredit the testimony he knew was coming from the other worker at the Shawmut Bank the night of the murder, Tracy Enzo.

"The blood she thought she saw on Mr. Anderson's sweatshirt was actually water he splashed on himself while mopping."

Next up for Jay Carney was the .25-caliber gun with Anderson's prints on it. Carney stated that, "The .25-

caliber gun was Mr. Andersons and he kept it in the van when he worked high crime areas like Lawrence. Mr. Prince had access to that gun while it was in the van."

Mr. Carney then went on to suggest that the 9 mm handgun that was found in the trash bag could also have been stolen by Prince or another member of the cleaning crew. Prince was one of the four man crew that cleaned the house in Manchester, NH where the gun was stolen. Carney additionally suggested that Prince could have planted the murder weapons in the Cherry and Webb Building because Anderson gave him the key, since Prince was scheduled to work there.

Attorney Carney went on to tell the jury that the Anderson home was searched by police the day after he was arrested, and no key was found. The key was in fact found by a family member three weeks later. Carney implied that when Prince came to visit the family to pay his respects, he planted the key.

Lastly, he simply denied that Robert Anderson was in love with Pam McEvoy. She was nothing more than an employee he gave gifts too because she was a single mother.

Prior to the Prosecutions opening statement, Judge Barton broke for lunch. In the courtroom hallway, Fred McAlary stated to reporters that in no way was Billy Prince connected to the crime.

****

In his opening statement, Fred McAlary began by stating, "That Mr. Prince was in no way linked to the murder or any crime. The Defense certainly twisted and turned all the facts to point the finger at him. But that's what defense attorneys do when they have no way out. The testimony will show that Billy had nothing to do with the murder of Amy Anderson. Mr. Prince who will be a prosecution witness, could not have killed Mrs. Anderson because he was locked in the basement at the time she was murdered."

McAlary went on to explain how Robert Anderson sent Prince and Enzo to the basement of the Shawmut Bank to do remediation work after it experienced water damage. He then took the elevator back to the first floor with his wife and locked the staircase door and disabled the elevator. Robert Anderson then walked his wife to the van where he killed her.

McAlary explained that the Andersons had a storybook life until the fall of 1993 when he met Pam McEvoy, a single mom living with her parents in North Andover, Ma. After starting a relationship with her, he began to think how he would get out of his marriage and preserve his wealth.

Prosecutor McAlary then told the story of how Robert Anderson planned and executed the killing.

"Mr. Anderson began to plan the killing a week before it happened when he told the manager of the Shawmut Bank that the furnace in the next door Cherry and Webb building might need to be fixed. He obtained a key to the building, which he never returned, and confirmed to the manager that this was in fact the case."

"The next day, Robert convinced his wife Amy to help him clean the Shawmut bank basement which had suffered damage from flooding. It was unusual for her to do this. After locking his employees in the basement, he asked his wife to go out for refreshments and walked her to the van where he attacked her, beating her with a five pound wrench about the head repeatedly which caused skull fragments to pierce her brain. He then brutally stabbed her in the face with a stolen four inch Phillips screwdriver and then sliced her with a carpet cutter which left a four inch gash across her cheek." As McAlary explained this, he held up the screwdriver in one hand and the wrench in another. "Mr. Anderson then returned to the bank and left Amy to die in the van."

"Upon returning to the bank basement via the elevator, Ms. Enzo, now of Texas, noticed a blood stain on Mr. Anderson's sweatshirt. He covered it up and then took the sweatshirt off in the bathroom. Mr. Anderson then rode the elevator to the first floor with Ms. Enzo where they began cleaning. After ten minutes, Mr. Anderson began to wonder what was taking his wife so long. He went to the back door and went out. He came back shortly and acted as he had discovered his beaten and dying wife for the first time. After she was transported to the hospital, Lawrence Police Detectives interviewed Anderson at the hospital. According to detectives, he reported in an unemotional way, that his wife might have been the victim of a street crime."

"But the facts didn't fit the story," McAlary continued.

"This is not a case of random urban violence. This is a case of deliberately premeditated murder. Robert Anderson inflicted those injuries that killed his wife Amy. There are numerous pieces of evidence that point to Mr. Anderson, and Mr. Anderson alone. Four days later, Lawrence Police Detective Mike Laird discovered a bag with the murder weapons, two guns and other items above a suspended ceiling in Cherry and Webb."

McAlary went on to explain how every item in that bag could be linked to Bob Anderson.

"Not only was the wrench, carpet cutter and screwdriver covered in blood, there was Amy Anderson's hair imbedded in the wrench which was proved conclusively by lab analysis. There was Mr. Anderson's fingerprint on the .25-caliber gun that he stole from a friend's home in Derry, and the other gun, a 9 mm handgun was stolen from a home in Manchester, NH which Bob Anderson had cleaned with a crew in January of 1994.

McAlary went on to explain how he will have testimony from State Lab experts who will confirm that the blood splatters on Mr. Anderson's jacket and sweatshirt were similar to splatters found in the van, and could only have come from the person who killed Amy Anderson, his wife, and the mother his children. Another lab expert will testify that the plaster dust found on Mr. Anderson's jacket could have only come from the ceiling tiles in Cherry and Webb where the murder weapons were found.

"The evidence will show beyond any shadow of a doubt, that Robert Anderson premeditated, and killed his wife, Amy Anderson."

Judge Barton adjourned court for the day and stated that tomorrow would begin with the prosecution calling its first witness.

Authors note: Much of the above came from an article in the Eagle Tribune written by Bill Murphy.

****

June 8, 1995
Thursday

The first witness that the prosecution called was Lawrence Patrolman Arthur Waller. After he was sworn in, Prosecutor McAlary began his questions.

After ascertaining that he was on duty that night and assigned to the mid-town sector, Patrolman Waller described how he received a call from dispatch to respond to the rear parking lot of the Shawmut Bank reference a serious assault. He also was advised that an ambulance was on the way.

"When I arrived at the scene, I saw the ServiceMaster van with the driver's side door open. The defendant, Robert Anderson was standing at the front of the van."

"Can you identify Robert Anderson?" asked Prosecutor McAlary.

"Yes he's at the defendants table wearing a gray suit and with a salt and pepper beard. He's seated next to Attorney Carney."

"Please go on officer."

Waller went on to explain that when he approached the driver's side door, Anderson, who identified himself to Waller as Amy's husband and the one who called, went into the van from the passenger's side and cradled Amy's head in his hands. He also stated that Amy was slumped to her right over the van's center console.

"Officer, did you notice if Mr. Anderson had any blood stains on his jacket."

"I noticed that his jacket was stained, but I couldn't tell if it was blood. It could have been."

"Go on officer. What else occurred?" McAlary asked.

"Mr. Anderson had his hands under the women's head and was cradling it. He was holding her head and talking to her. She was still breathing, but having a hard time. She was gurgling and blowing bubbles. Just at this time, the ambulance arrived."

Waller then went on to say how he asked Mr. Anderson some questions and learned there were two of his employees in the Shawmut bank, cleaning. Waller was also told by Anderson he didn't know who did this and didn't see anything.

Waller testified that in a short time, Detective Burokas arrived on the scene along with a supervisor and two other officers.

"Mrs. Anderson was in bad shape and Mr. Anderson accompanied her in the ambulance to the Lawrence General Hospital."

On cross-examination Carney had Officer Waller re-affirm that he wasn't able to tell that the stains on Robert Anderson's jacket were blood, and they could have been dirt stains. Waller also couldn't tell if Anderson's sweatshirt was stained.

****

The next person the prosecution called was Mary Lucas, a friend of the Andersons who lived close to the Andersons in Salem, NH. She confirmed she did the bookkeeping for Anderson's business and was at the hospital the night of the murder. When asked, she testified "that Robert did not act like a man whose wife was just beaten up."

"I found him to be very unemotional. He didn't show any signs of being emotionally hurt."

Mary Lucas went on to testify that Mr. Anderson, who was usually upbeat became unhappy in the fall of 1993 when Pam McEvoy began working for him. Mrs. Lucas also declared that Robert Anderson began running up credit card expenses at restaurants, hotels and ski facilities from fall of 1993 to February of 1994.

"Mr. Anderson seemed unfocused at that time and one of the things that was unusual was that he didn't always return customer's phone calls."

On cross-examination, Attorney Carney asked Mrs. Lucas if she had any formal training in behavioral psychology or any type of training in interpreting body language.

"No I don't."

"So isn't possible Mrs. Lucas that what you described as Mr. Anderson not acting like someone whose wife had just been assaulted, could actually have been shock and incomprehension?"

After a moment's hesitation, "Well, I guess so."

Carney's next line of questioning involved Mr. Anderson's excessive credit card use.

"These credit card receipts at restaurants, could they have been customers?

"Yes."

"And could some of the travel expenses been for soliciting more customers."

"Yes."

"Mrs. Lucas, is it possible that these could have been visits to clients?"

"Yes, but on the ski trip he was accompanied by Pam McEvoy."

"Wasn't she a marketing specialist?" Carney asked.

"Well, that's the title she was given. She was part-time and she was paid three-hundred dollars per week. I don't really know what she did besides go with Robert on trips."

"Thank you. No further questions."

On re-direct McAlary asked two questions.

"Mrs. Lucas, were you able to tell how many hotel rooms that Mr. Anderson rented when he was on these business trips with Ms. McEvoy?"

"Yes, I was able to tell from the receipts he gave me."

"How many rooms did he rent when she was with him?"

"Just one."

"Thank you."

****

The next person on the stand was Amy's mother. Her answer to the first question was a break for the defense. When she was asked about Mr. Anderson's demeanor at the hospital, she said that it was someone who appeared to be in a state of shock.

Amy's Mother then testified that her daughter and Mr. Anderson seemed to get along very well until January of 1994.

"Amy spoke very harshly of her husband from mid-January until the day she was killed in late February."

"Did they argue much," McAlary asked,

"It seemed like all the time but never in front of the children, and she still did what he asked of her, like going to help him that night."

Amy's mother's voice cracked and she began to cry when she described how her daughter left to go clean the bank with her husband February 26.

"She put her winter jacket on and said 'Mom, I should be home by 8 o'clock.'"

"No further questions," McAlary said.

"Mr. Carney," Judge Barton said.

"No questions your honor."

Judge Barton said, "You may step down ma'am and thank you. I know that was difficult."

Court was then adjourned for the day.

The Eagle Tribune took note of the fact that Robert Anderson's good friend and confidant, Ray Corliss, was in the court room. After Ray left Salem High as the Principle in 1983, he worked in the insurance business until 1994 when he returned as principle to Salem High School. He was still principle during the trial and still couldn't believe that his friend Robert Anderson killed his wife Amy.

****

After court was adjourned, the jury foreman, John Williams, informed the bailiff that he needed to see Judge Barton.

The judge agreed to meet him in his chambers while also summonsing Attorney's McAlary and Carney.

Williams informed Judge Barton that one of the

witnesses that day, Mary Lucas, used to babysit his children about 30 years ago when she was a student at Merrimack College in North Andover, Ma. The judge asked Williams a number of questions concerning his impartiality and if he told any of the other jurors this. When Williams assured the judge that he can remain impartial and had told no one about how he knew Mary Lucas, the Judge decided that he could remain on the jury as its foreman.

Attorney Carney objected to this but was overruled by Judge Barton.

****

It was announced that day that Mathew Stuart, Charles Stuarts bother who went to the police and said that it was Charles who murdered his wife Carol in 1989, was going to be paroled later in the month of June. He had been incarcerated since 1991 at the Franklin County House of Correction in Greenfield, Ma.

****

June 9, 1995
Friday

The day started with the testimony of Doctor Edward Covey, the neurosurgeon who was on call the night Amy Anderson was murdered.

His testimony was that Amy Anderson's wounds were not survivable and he was surprised that she had lived until the following morning. Her heartbeat was as low as fourteen beats per minute.

"When she first came in, we put a blood drip on her and she was intubated. She had a tremendous amount of blood loss and probably the reason why she didn't die from blood loss in the van that night was the sub-freezing weather that helped the blood to coagulate. Before operating, we had to shave her head. The wounds were extensive. The left side of her head was hit with a heavy object four or five times with a lot of force. Skull fragments pierced her brain. If she did survive, her speech would have been severely impaired along with reasoning and analytical ability. But as I said previously, these wounds were not survivable."

"Thank you doctor."

Attorney Carney had no questions for the doctor on cross-examination.

****

William Prince took the stand next, the former student and gymnast of Robert Anderson who was hired by Anderson in 1989 after Prince was honorably discharged by the marines.

After being sworn in, McAlary asked William Prince how he knew the Andersons. Prince said he first met Mr. Anderson his freshman year in high school when Anderson was Prince's Gym teacher. He was later his gymnastic coach.

He met Amy Anderson his freshman year too, since she was Prince's English teacher. Prince stated that while she was a really good teacher, he had difficulty handling her class because she was demanding, but very helpful and kind towards her students.

McAlary then asked Prince questions concerning the night Amy Anderson was murdered. Prince stated that he and Tracy Enzo had met the Anderson's at the Shawmut bank parking lot a little after 6 PM. He and Tracy Enzo had first gone to the office at 4 Raymond Avenue in Salem, and took a company vehicle. They subsequently met the Anderson's at the Shawmut bank. Prince then testified how he went to the van the Anderson's drove and he, Tracy and Robert Anderson brought the cleaning materials to the bank and unlocked the door.

"Once you were in the bank, did Mr. Anderson lock any doors?

"No he didn't, but he told us we would be working in the basement and we couldn't use the stairs because the doors were locked and it would set off the alarm if we tried."

"What happened next?

"We got in the elevator and went into the basement."

"Why there?"

"Shawmut bank was one of our accounts, and they had experienced water damage earlier in the week from a burst pipe and we needed to clean up. That would include disinfecting the basement, disperse anti-mold solution, and then place and start heaters and fans in the basement for a couple of days."

"Please go on."

"Mr. Anderson then asked his wife if she would go out and get us some coffee or anything. I was kind of surprised because we weren't going to be there that long. Both Tracy and I said we didn't want anything but Mr. Anderson insisted. He and his wife then went up the elevator. Mr. Anderson said he was going to walk his wife to the van."

"Did she say anything?"

"She said something like 'no need, the van is just outside the back door.' Mr. Anderson then said he would prefer to do it since there's a lot of violence in Lawrence."

"After they left, did you have occasion to try the elevator?"

"Yes. I told Tracy I forgot some cleaning supplies upstairs. I pushed the up button for the elevator but nothing happened. After a minute I pushed it a couple of more times. I figured it was either broken or maybe Mr. Anderson had stopped it on the first floor."

"When did Mr. Anderson come back and what happened."

"In about ten to fifteen minutes, we heard footsteps upstairs and then the elevator started down. Mr. Anderson got out of it and told Tracy to come with him, they were going to do the weekly cleaning upstairs."

"What happened next?"

"In about fifteen minutes or so, I heard yelling from upstairs from Mr. Anderson."

"What did you do?"

"I got in the elevator and went to the first floor where Tracy and Mr. Anderson were. He was talking really loud and fast into the phone and he said his wife had gotten beat up and the ambulance had to hurry."

"Did you go outside at all?"

"Yes. After Mr. Anderson got off of the phone. I asked, 'What happened?' He told me that Amy was in bad shape out in the van. We then both went out to the van."

"What did you see?"

"I saw blood everywhere and I saw Mrs. Anderson in the van. She looked really bad and I couldn't stand it. I ran back into the bank and I told Tracy not to go out there since Mrs. Anderson was in really bad shape."

"Mr. Prince, when you heard Mr. Anderson yelling, you said you went up in the elevator?"

"Yes."

"Was this the first time you left the basement since you got there?"

"That's correct. I wasn't able to leave the basement since the elevator wasn't responding and the door to the stairs was locked."

"And the other worker, Tracy Enzo, was she with you?"

"Yes, until Mr. Anderson came and told her to come to the first floor with her, then I was alone for around fifteen minutes and I only left the basement when I heard Mr. Anderson yelling."

"Thank you,"

"The Defense attorney, Mr. Carney, said in his opening statement that Mr. Anderson gave you the key to the building next door, Cherry and Webb, and that you were going to be responsible for cleaning the place."

"That's just not true. I never knew anything about Cherry and Webb and I've never been in the building, let alone have the key."

"Thank you Mr. Prince. Attorney Carney also suggested the bloody key to Cherry and Webb may have been planted by you in the Anderson house when you came to offer condolences."

"That's not true either. I went over to the Anderson house on Monday night and the house was full of people. They invited me in but I never went past the doorway because there were so many people and I didn't want to intrude. Amy Anderson was very popular. I offered my condolences and left."

"Thank you."

"Mr. Prince you heard of the .25-caliber handgun that was found with the murder weapons."

"Yes."

"Did you ever see or handle that gun."

"No sir. I never saw the gun, much less handle it."

"Thank you Mr. Prince. No further questions."

****

Attorney Carney walked towards the witness box.

"Mr. Prince, you testified that Mr. Anderson said the doors to the stairway leading to the basement were locked."

"Yes sir."

"Did you ever check the door on the first floor to see if it was locked?"

"No I didn't."

"When you were down in the basement working, was there a door to the stairway leading upstairs?"

"Yes there was."

"Did you check to see if that was locked?"

"I did not."

"Did you see your co-worker Tracy Enzo check either door?"

"I didn't see her check either door."

"So you have no personal knowledge that the door was lock?"

"That's correct."

"Thank you."

Attorney Carney continued, "When Mr. Anderson came back from walking his wife to the van, he came down to the basement, and then he and Tracy Enzo took the elevator back to the first floor to clean. Is that correct?"

"To the best of my memory, yes."

"Where were they cleaning?"

"I believe it was the lobby of the bank."

"Have you cleaned the bank lobby in previous visits?

"Yes I have."

"Where are the stairs leading to go downstairs from the lobby?"

"As you walk into the bank, there are a set of double doors before you enter the lobby. The stairs leading to the basement are on your left after you go through the first door."

"So if you're cleaning the lobby, aren't there blind spots in the lobby where you wouldn't be able to see the door leading to the basement stairs?"

After a moment's hesitation, Prince replied, "Yes that's true, there are some area's in the lobby where you wouldn't see that door."

"So if you're cleaning the lobby in those areas," Carny said, "it's possible you wouldn't be able to see anyone coming up and going through the door, or going through the door and going down."

"Yea, I guess so."
"No further questions."

****

On redirect McAlary asked several questions.

"Mr. Prince, just to reiterate, the only time you came up from the basement was after you heard Mr. Anderson yelling and it was by the elevator. Is that correct?"

"Yes it is."

"McAlary then took a yellow Husky tool bag from the prosecution's table and handed it to Bill Prince.

"Mr. Prince, do you recognize this bag?"

"Yes, it's my tool bag, I wrote my name in it."

"Do you carry this around with you on jobs?"

"Yes I do."

"Thank you."

Judge Barton then adjourned court for the day and weekend.

"Court will resume Monday at 9 AM.

"All rise."

As Jay Carney was leaving court, he wondered what the significance of the tool bag was.

****

June 12, 1995
Monday

Judge Barton walked into court promptly at 9 AM on Monday morning.

"Attorney McAlary, please call your next witness."

The next witness was David Coe, the chemist for the state lab.

"Mr. Coe, did you provide a blood analysis of the blood on the five pound wrench that was the murder weapon, and the jacket worn on the night of the murder by Mr. Anderson."

"Yes."

"Can you briefly explain, in layman's terms, how DNA analysis works?"

"DNA can be used to identify individuals on the basis of their unique genetic makeup, and by unique, you alone have this makeup. Relatives have shared make ups, but not identical. Genome is the term we used for someone's DNA's makeup. The analysis captures all of the 6 billion markers, known as nucleotides, in a genome which we call profiling or genetic fingerprinting. It reveals variations in the genetic code that, taken together, constitute, again, an individual's unique DNA profile. Even identical twins have subtle differences. Only one-hundred micrograms is needed for a DNA sample."

"What did you find Mr. Coe?"

"I compared the blood on the jacket and wrench, and there also were imbedded hairs on the wrench, to hairs found on Mrs. Anderson's hairbrush from her house, and they were identical."

"What are the odds of this being a mistake?"
"About a billion to one."
"How many tests did you run Mr. Coe?"
"On murder cases, we always do it twice."

"Did you get the same results each time?
"I did."
"Thank you sir."

Attorney Carney had no questions on cross.

Judge Barton then announced that court would be adjourned until tomorrow so that the jurors may tour the Shawmut Bank and Cherry and Webb buildings and parking lot.

There were accompanied by Sherriff deputies and the prosecuting and defense attorneys.

****

During the tour of the bank, the defense team got a lucky break. After half the jury went down the elevator, the elevator got stuck. During this time, one of the deputies went to find the bank manager to unlock the doors leading to the basement. While the deputy was away, one of the jurors tried the door to the basement, and it was unlocked. They went down the stairs and found that the door at the bottom of the stairs that opened to the basement, was also unlocked.

This added some credence to the defense's contention that William Prince had the opportunity to leave the basement.

****

On Friday June 9th, Judge Ito ruled that the jury may see over forty photos of the Nicole Brown Simpson and Ron Goldman murder scene in addition to the autopsy photos. About three-quarters of the way through viewing the photos, one of the jurors became sick and had to run out of the court room. Judge Ito adjourned court for the day. On Monday, the rest of the photos, which were being displayed on an easel, were moved back three feet from the jury.

****

June 13, 1995
Tuesday

Judge Barton had previously ruled that the jurors in the Anderson murder case may view the crime scene and autopsy photos.

The first witness of the day was Dr. Leonard Atkins from the Massachusetts Medical Examiner's office who performed the autopsy on Amy Anderson. The photos were on an easel and he was allowed to speak outside the witness box to display the photos as he was speaking. Prosecutor McAlary cautioned everyone that the photographs would be particularly graphic and disturbing.

Dr. Leonard testified that Amy's face was slashed, stabbed and bludgeoned and it bordered on mutilation.

He further testified that she was beaten so brutally, that it left her head severely swollen, such that it appeared to belong to a much larger woman.

As Dr. Leonard was testifying, he was showing the jury and court room observers pictures of the crime scene and autopsy. There were audible gasps from the jury and many sobs from the courtroom.

"Dr. Leonard, can you described what kind of objects would have caused these wounds?"

"Yes. The face would have been slashed with a very sharp instrument, the stab wounds would have been caused by a poking instrument that was not sharp, and a heavy blunt object was used to hit her on the head, neck and shoulders."

Fred McAlary then went to the prosecutor's table and grabbed three bloody objects.

The first object McAlary held up was a carpet cutting tool.

"Dr. Leonard, would this carpet cutter be capable of causing the wounds to Amy Anderson's face?"

"Yes it would. The carpet razor is extremely sharp. The murderer would have had no problem making the four slashes that were on her face and head. They were all extremely injurious. One almost cut her left ear in half, another accounted for a three inch cut on her chin. There was a four inch gash that ran from her cheek to her neck and a four and one-half inch gas on the back of her head."

"Dr Leonard, would this Phillips screwdriver be capable of the stabbing wounds you described."

"Yes it would. Amy Anderson was stabbed several times near the left temple and ear."

"And lastly Doctor, would this five pound wrench be capable of the bludgeoning wounds you described?"

"Yes it would. The wrench would have had no problem causing the skull fractures that pierced her brain and the massive bruises on her shoulder and neck. One of the blows caused a ten inch crack that ran from her left ear to the back of her head. It was truly amazing that she lasted until the next morning."

"No further questions."

Attorney Carney had no questions and since there were very few dry eyes in the court room, Judge Barton called for a thirty minute recess.

****

During the recess, Prosecutor McAlary had occasion to talk to a number of reporters. He told them that Robert Anderson was an immediate suspect since the attack had the hallmarks of an act of extreme rage. Only later did police realize that it was not spontaneous, but a planned and premeditated act.

****

The next witness was the other ServiceMaster employee who worked the night Amy Anderson was murdered, Tracy Enzo.

Tracy testified that when she worked for the Anderson's, she lived in Raymond, NH, but eventually moved to Texas, where she was raised as a child. She did this to get away from the publicity and memories of the murder. The state of Massachusetts paid for her transportation cost from Texas in addition to housing and meals.

"Mrs. Enzo, were you working for Robert Anderson the night that Amy Anderson was murdered?"

"Yes I was. I met Billy at the office a little before 6 PM where we grabbed a company vehicle and drove to the Shawmut bank in Lawrence where we met the Anderson's."

"And by Billy, you mean William Prince?"

"Yes."

"Can you please describe to the court the events of that night?"

"Well, we got to the bank about five minutes before the Andersons. It was cold with really light snow. When we went in the bank we went downstairs to the basement by using the elevator."

"Mrs. Enzo, once you entered the bank, did Mr. Anderson lock the entrance door behind him?"

"No he didn't."

"Was that unusual?"

"Yes it was. He has keys to all the businesses we clean, and he always locks the door behind him, and if we're cleaning a business without him, he tells us to always lock the door behind us."

"Did Mr. Anderson say anything about the stairs leading to the basement?"

"Yes. He told us not to use the stairs because it would set off the alarm and the door to the stairs were locked anyway."

"Did all four of you go down to the basement?"

"Yes."

"And once you got to the basement, what happened."

"Mr. Anderson then asked us if we needed anything to eat or drink. Amy would go out to get it"

"Did you find this unusual?"

"Yes because we were only going to be there a short time. Probably an hour, no more than two."

"Go on please."

"Mr. Anderson then said that he would walk Amy to the van."

"Did Amy Anderson say anything?"

"She said something like, you don't have too. But Mr. Anderson said that he would because Lawrence is a violent city."

"Did you notice many people walking about in Lawrence as you and Mr. Prince drove to the bank?"

"There was hardly anyone on the roads and no one walking. It was really cold and there were snow flurries."

"Thank you. After the Andersons left the basement what happened?"

"In a few minutes, Billy said that he forgot some supplies upstairs and pushed the elevator button. But it never came down. I tried it a few times too with no luck over about a five minute period."

"About what time was this?"

"It was around 6:30."

"When did Mr. Anderson return?"

"He was gone awhile, about ten to fifteen minutes."

"When he came back, where were you?"

"I was working just outside the elevator and Billy was in another room cleaning."

"Did you see anything unusual?"

"Yes. On Mr. Anderson's sweatshirt, by the right collar, there was a blood stain and I pointed it out to him. I asked 'why is there blood on your sweatshirt?'"

"What did he say or do."

"He kind of looked down at it and said, 'oh, don't worry about that,' and covered it up with his hand. He then went back into the elevator and went upstairs."

"Please go on."

"I then spoke to Billy and told him about the stain. I told him that I have a weird feeling about this and something is wrong, something is not right here. Billy then said, 'yea, that's a little weird.' I then told Billy maybe they were fooling around upstairs and Amy got a little bit carried away. We then went back to cleaning."

"What happened next?"

"In a few minutes, Mr. Anderson came back downstairs and told me to come upstairs with him to clean the lobby. He told Billy to come up after he was done."

"Did he still have the sweatshirt on?"

"Yes but there was a wet spot where the blood stain was. I guessed that he cleaned it up."

"Go on please."

"We went upstairs and started cleaning the lobby. In about, I guess ten minutes, Mr. Anderson said something to the extent that 'I wonder where Amy is?' I'm going to go outside and check.' He came back in screaming that his wife got beat up. He went to the phone and called the police. He was screaming into the phone and talking real fast. Billy must have heard him so he came up in the elevator just as Mr. Anderson hung up. Billy asked what was going on and Mr. Anderson said that his wife was beat up and bloody in the van. They then both ran outside."

"Go on."

"Billy came back in a little while and he told me not to go out there. There was blood everywhere. The police and ambulance came and Amy was taken to the hospital. Mr. Anderson went with her in the ambulance. Some

Lawrence detectives interviewed us about what happened before Mr. Anderson went out to see where Amy was."

"Did you tell any of the detectives about the bloodstain on Mr. Anderson's sweatshirt?"

"Yes. I believe it was detective McDonald."

"Thank you Mrs. Enzo. No further questions."

****

A brief recess was called before attorney Carney began his cross-examination of Tracy Enzo.

"Mrs. Enzo, you testified that when you entered the bank with Robert and Amy Anderson, Robert didn't lock the door. Is that correct."

"Yes."

"You also testified that was unusual?"

"Yes."

"Can you say beyond a reasonable doubt that Mr. Anderson locked every door of every business he entered to clean? Could he have left some doors unlocked?"

"It's possible."

"So it's possible that he didn't always lock doors behind him."

"Yes."

"Thank you. You also testified that Mr. Anderson said the doors to the stairs leading to the basement were locked."

"Yes."

"Mrs. Enzo, did you check either the door at the top of the stairs or bottom to see if they were locked?"

"No I didn't."

"So it's possible that they could've been unlocked and the stairwell leading to the outside back door was accessible?"

"Yes, it's possible."

After attorney Carney consulted his notes, he continued.

"Mrs. Enzo, you also testified that you were downstairs with Mr. Prince for over fifteen minutes?"

"Yes."

"Was Mr. Prince visible to you all that time?"

"No he wasn't. I was in one room cleaning and he was in another."

"Was he in a room that was closer to the stairs than you?"

"Yes, the stairs were right next to the door to his room."

"Was he out of your sight for more than ten minutes?"

"Yes. I guess so."

"So if the stairway doors were unlocked, he could have left and returned within ten minutes without you knowing. Is that possible."

"I guess it's possible."

"Just to clarify, you're testifying that it was possible for Mr. Prince to leave the basement and you wouldn't have known."

"Yes."

"Thank you. You testified earlier that you commented to Mr. Prince that 'maybe they were fooling around up stairs and Amy got carried away?' And by they, you meant Amy and Bob Anderson?"

"Yes."

"So would you agree that you thought they loved each other?"

"I guess you could say that."

"One last question. You testified that you thought there was a blood stain on Bob Anderson's sweatshirt. Were you one-hundred percent positive? Could it have been some other stain?"

After hesitating, Emro replied, "Possibly."

"Thank you. No further questions."

On redirect, prosecutor McAlary had only one question for Tracy Enzo. When he left the prosecution table he had a small yellow Husky tool bag with him.

"Mrs. Enzo, do you recognize this bag?"

"Yes, it looks like the tool bag that Billy always carried around with him."

"Were there ever any tools hanging out of this bag?"

"Not that I can remember. Billy was always very neat."

McAlary walked backed to the prosecutors table and grabbed one of the murder weapons, the five pound adjustable wrench and handed both the wrench and bag to Tracy Enzo.

"Mrs. Enzo can you try and put this wrench into the bag?"

"It won't fit."

"So the only way it could be carried in the bag is if it was hanging out."

"Correct."

"And did you notice any tools hanging out of his bag on the night of Amy's murder?"

"No I did not."

"Thank You.

Judge Barton adjourned court for the day.

****

During the OJ Simpson trial, the prosecution introduced a pair of leather gloves that were drenched in blood from the murder scene of Nicole Brown Smith and Ron Goldman. The prosecution said that these gloves were OJ Simpsons according to one of the two prosecutors, Chris Darden. It seemed like a slam dunk until Simpson's lawyer Johnnie Cochran (one of Simpson's three dream team lawyers) had Simpson try on the gloves. Darden didn't object and never pointed out to the jury that when wet, either with water or blood, leather would shrink. As can be surmised, the gloves were too small for Simpson which led to the famous quote by Cochran, "If it does not fit, you must acquit."

The Simpson case continued for another three months but many courtroom observers and legal experts claimed that this was the turning point of the trial.

Lead prosecutor, Marcia Clark seemed to be watching her case fall apart and she supposedly commented to a friend of hers, "Do you even think we have a chance."

****

June 14, 1995
Wednesday

Court was called to session promptly at 9 AM and the prosecutions first witness of the day was Judith Smith, the manager of the Shawmut bank on Essex Street in Lawrence.

After being sworn in, Mrs. Smith testified that she was the manager of the bank and she had known Mr. Anderson since his franchise had been cleaning the bank for several years. When Cherry and Webb went out of business next door to the bank, Shawmut became the caretakers of the building.

"Mrs. Smith, did you ever have occasion to give Mr. Anderson the key to Cherry and Webb?"

"Yes I did."

"Can you relate to the court how that happened to come about?"

"Mr. Anderson told me that there was a dust problem in our building that he thought was being caused by the boiler in the deserted Cherry and Webb building since the two buildings are connected. He then asked for the key to that building."

"Was it given to him?"

"Initially it was given to him by our facilities director who had the key. My facilities director then went into the building with him."

"What happened next?"

"They came back to my office and Mr. Anderson said that the boiler was the problem and that he, Mr. Anderson, said he could take care of it."

"I told him that would be fine and we scheduled a day the following week that he could fix it."

"Please continue."

"Mr. Anderson then asked if he could have the key again since he forgot something in the boiler room. I had Gary give him the key."

"Did you ever get it back?"

"No. We forgot all about it since we were closing. When the police came the following week and asked to search the building, we were lucky that we had a spare key."

"And to your knowledge, you never got the key back from Mr. Anderson."

"That's correct."

"No further questions."

****

"Mrs. Smith," asked Jay Carney, "do you know what happened to that key that you said you never received back from Robert Anderson?"

"No I don't."

"So you really don't know if he either gave it to another person who worked for him, or if it was taken from him by another worker."

"No I don't."

"Thank you. No further questions."

****

The anticipation of the next witness testifying had the courtroom packed. It was Pam McEvoy who was allegedly the love interest of Robert Anderson. She now lived in Alexandria, Va. Having moved there not long after the murder. The state of Massachusetts also paid for her travel, food and lodging expenses from Virginia.

After taking the stand, Pam McEvoy was sworn in and identified herself, prosecutor McAlary began his questioning.

"Ms. McEvoy, what do you do for work?"

"I work in retail."

"What specifically."

"I sell cosmetics."

"Did you have occasion to meet the defendant in early October of 1993."

"Yes. He came to my mother's apartment in North Andover, where I also lived, to inspect the cleaning job that some of his workers did. My mother had complained that it wasn't done to her liking."

"And what happened after his inspection."

"He said he would send his best crew over first thing the next morning and he would come by before noon to personally inspect it."

"And did that happen."

"Yes, his crew was there at nine and he came by shortly before noon."

"What happened when he came by?"

"He asked if I was happy with the job, which I was, and then said he wanted to make it up to me for the inconvenience. He gave me a gift and asked to take me out to lunch."

"What was the gift and did you go out to lunch?"

"The gift was jewelry, I think earrings, and we did go out to lunch."

"What did you discuss at lunch?"

"He said something to the extent that his business was doing well but that he wasn't happy in his marriage. I told him that I was divorced and it was hard making ends meet as a single mother. But I was lucky that I lived with my parents from a financial point of view, and they loved babysitting for my son."

"Did you have lunch with him again?"

"Yes, two other times that week."

"Did Mr. Anderson give you gifts at those lunches?"

"Yes he did."

"Did anything else happen."

"Yes he offered me a job."

"What was the job and how much was he willing to pay you."

"It was a part-time job as a marketing specialist and he offered me $300 per week."

"Were you able to keep your other job as a cosmetic saleswoman?"

"Yes I was. He said that I would be able to work around my job in retail.

"Did you accept the job?"

"Yes I did."

"When did you start?"

"The following week."

"And what were your duties."

"Primarily, nothing. I was his travelling companion every time I worked."

"How often did you work?"

"Two or three days a week for about five to six hours a day."

"Did Mr. Anderson give you any special instructions on what to wear?"

"Yes. "

"What were they?"

"He said that when we go to see a client or prospective client, I should wear a short dress and high heels and cross my legs a lot because that's what men like and that's what gets business."

"And did you?"

"Yes, I thought that was relatively harmless."

"How did your relationship develop?"

"It wasn't really a relationship. He continued to take me to lunch and give me gifts."

"Was it a sexual relationship?"

"No, though he wanted it to be. I told him I had a boyfriend."

"And what did he say to that."

"Well, he was frustrated and he said that at some point 'he will have me.'"

"Did he ever talk about his marriage?"

"Yes. He said he and his wife were more like best friends and he would divorce his wife to be with me. I believe she asked him if he was having an affair with me and he said no."

"Did he do anything special on Christmas for you?"

"We each spent Christmas with our families. But he mentioned to me that in his family they do the twenty-four days of Christmas, where he and his wife give their kids little gifts beginning December 1st right up until Christmas day."

"Did Mr. Anderson do the twenty four days of Christmas with you?"

"Yes he did. We had lunch every day and I got gifts every day."

"What were some of these gifts?"

"A gift card to Demoulas for $300, ballet tickets, more jewelry, and a $500 gift certificate and a round trip plane ticket to Colorado where I could see my other child. There was also perfume, teddy bears, candles and sweatshirts. We also went skiing to Loon Mountain and he paid for everything."

"Was that trip on a day you usually work?"

"Yes."

"And you continued to get paid $300 per week all this time?"

"Yes, until shortly after Mrs. Anderson was killed and he was arrested."

"And did you accept all these gifts?"

"Yes. I thought that if he was stupid enough to give me all these gifts, I'm going to be smart enough to take them."

"Did you ever spend the night with Mr. Anderson?"

"Yes. We went on a training trip to Worcester, Ma that ServiceMaster was sponsoring."

"Please describe the trip and what happened?"

"We drove to Worcester in the morning and after the training that day, we stopped at a store and he bought some whiskey, vodka and orange juice. We then went to the Marriot hotel where Robert told me that he only rented one hotel room. I told him I wanted my own room, but he said he was paying for it. I then told him that I hoped there were separate beds in the room and he said there was only one."

"What happened that evening please?"

"We went to dinner, had a few drinks in the lounge and played some pool."

"What happened when you went back to the room?"

"It was an awkward night. I put on sweatpants and a shirt and was reading a book in bed. He came to bed in only his underwear and said to me 'I know that's not what you normally wear to bed.' I just continued to read my book. When we woke up the next morning he was still unhappy and took me home. We didn't go to the second day of the training seminar."

"Thank you. And to reiterate, you never had sex with Mr. Anderson?"

"That's correct. We never had sex and I told him a number of times I had a boyfriend and just wanted to be friends."

"Did you continue to see Mr. Anderson outside of work after the training day?"

"Yes. A couple of nights later we had dinner at the Bay Tower room in Boston."

"Did he continue to give you gifts?"

"Yes. The biggest gift he gave me was in mid-January."

"What was it?"

"His wife and he had signed a cashier's check for $10,000 which he converted to a $10,000 Treasury bond made out to him and me. He said that if his business had a good year I would get the bond as a bonus. I asked him wouldn't Amy be mad and he said probably."

"Where was this bond kept?"

"It was in a safety deposit box at his bank in addition to $35,000 in cash."

"Thank you. Let's continue. Ms. McEvoy, did Mr. Anderson pay to have your car repaired?"

"Yes. About four or five times."

"Did Mr. Anderson make an offer to you concerning your living arrangements?"

"Yes. At one point I expressed a desire to move out of my parent's apartment in the Royal Crest complex in North Andover. He said that he would kick one of his tenants out and I could live there."

"Was there anything else he offered concerning your living arrangements?"

"Yes. He also offered to buy a home for me and I could make the mortgage payments to him."

"When did he make this offer?"

"Shortly before Mrs. Anderson's murder."

"Were there any other gifts in February?"

"Yes, a $380 television set."

"Did he make any arrangements with you concerning his business?"

"Yes. He told me that he had a tumor behind his eye that was inoperable since the operation would leave him blind, and that he had set up a trust fund for me and my son upon his death. He told me the fund would pay me $5,000 annually for five years and then I would become the owner of the cleaning company. I asked him what about Amy and the kids and he said they were already taken care of."

"Ms. McEvoy, did Mr. Anderson ever tell you he loved you?"

"Yes."

"When did he first tell you that he loved you?"

"It was sometime in mid-November."

"Did he continue to tell you that he loved you?"

"Yes, numerous times."

"Would you say he told you that weekly?"

"Usually two or three times a week."

"When was the last time he told you he loved you?"

"A couple of days before Mrs. Anderson was murdered."

"Did you ever tell Mr. Anderson you loved him?"

"Never," Pam McEvoy said with particular emphasis.

"Thank you Ms. McEvoy. No further questions."

Judge Barton adjourned court for the day and attorney Carney would begin his cross examination the following day.

Authors note: It appears that Robert Anderson's story of an inoperable tumor behind his eye was a fabrication.

****

After court was recessed, both attorneys spoke to the press outside the courtroom. Attorney McAlary stated that he thought "Pam McEvoy was a devastating witness."

Attorney Carney stated, "I am too much of a gentleman to comment on her character."

****

June 15, 1995
Thursday

The day began with the cross-examination of Pam McEvoy by attorney Carney.

"Ms. McEvoy, is it safe to say that you never, ever led Robert Anderson to believe that even if he weren't married, he could have a relationship with you?"

"That's a fair statement."

"And you testified that you gave Mr. Anderson nothing in return for your $300 per week job outside of being his travelling companion?"

"That's correct."

"Did you ever answer any phones for him?"

"No."

"Did you ever do any book keeping for the business?"

"No."

"Your title was that of a marketing specialist?"

"Yes."

"Did you ever put any advertising adds together?"

"No."

"Did you ever talk to newspapers, radio stations or any other type of media concerning promoting the business?"

"No."

"Thank you. And you said you had a boyfriend the entire time you worked for Robert Anderson. Is that correct."

"Yes."

"Would you be considered Robert Anderson's lover?"

"Absolutely not."

"Did you have sexual intimacy of any type with Robert?"

"Never."

"Were you a prostitute at this time?"

"No."

"And even though you received many gifts at this time, you never gave him anything in return?"

"No. He received nothing from me."

"Would you agree that Mr. Anderson spent more of his waking time with you socially than his wife?"

"Possibly, yes."

"And did Robert take you to the ballet and posh Boston restaurants because his social life was dull at home?"

"Actually, no. He said he hated the ballet and he hated country music. He also took me to a Garth Brooks concert."

It appeared to observers that this was not the answer that Jay Carney had expected.

Jay Carney changed tack and went to the defense table and showed McEvoy a police report.

"Ms. McEvoy is this police report an accurate representation of what you told Detective Rheault of Salem, NH and Trooper Zuk?"

"Yes it is," McEvoy said after reading the report.

"Mr. Anderson did say to me that he would never leave his wife and I reported that to detectives," she added.

"Ms. McEvoy, you previously testified that you thought Robert Anderson was stupid?"

"He's not a stupid man. I believe it was a dumb thing to do. He just kept giving me gifts and money."

"Ms. McEvoy, did Robert ever ask you why you spurned his advances?"

"Yes, he once asked me would I go out with him if he was younger."

"And what was your response?"

"I said no because you're too obnoxious."

"No further questions."

Prosecutor McAlary had no questions on redirect.

Pam McEvoy was excused from the stand and she had to walk by both the Anderson and Amy's family as she was leaving the courtroom. As she did, she held her head high. As she opened the door to leave the courtroom she began to sob.

She was followed out of the courtroom by a man in his twenties believed to be her boyfriend.

Authors note: like the Charles Stuart murder case, investigators remain split as to whether there was a sexual relationship between Robert Anderson and Pam McEvoy.

****

After a brief recess, Detective Fred Rheault of the Salem, NH Police Department was called to the stand by the prosecutor. After being sworn in and identifying himself McAlary began his questions of the detective.

"Detective Rheault, did you take part in the investigation and arrest of Robert Anderson?"

"Yes."

"And after Mr. Anderson was arrested, did you have occasion to speak with attorney James Carpenito?"

"Yes."

"Please explain to the court the circumstances of that call."

"After we arrested Mr. Anderson he was booked at the station and was going to be arraigned the following day at Salem District Court on a Fugitive from Justice Warrant out of Massachusetts. We, the Lawrence Police, Mass

State Police and Salem PD detectives, were concerned about him making bail and possibly leaving the state."

"Why were you concerned about Mr. Anderson leaving the state?"

"We received information from a confidential informant of Trooper Zuk that he was planning a ski trip with Ms. McEvoy the day after the funeral."

"What did you do then Detective?"

"I contacted Attorney James Carpenito who I knew was Amy's family lawyer."

"Are you aware of what he did?"

"Yes, he put a lien on Mr. Anderson's assets pending a wrongful death suit. As a result of this, Mr. Anderson would not be able to post bail unless it was from a bail bondsman or some other third person."

"Are you aware of other actions Attorney Carpenito took?"

"Yes. As a result of my investigation, I learned that Mr. Anderson may have a safety deposit box in a local bank containing cash and securities. Attorney Carpenito had attached those assets pending a wrongful death lawsuit. Attorney Carpenito also served subpoenas to nine local banks in the event there was more than one box."

"And did you find any safety deposit boxes belonging to Mr. Anderson."

"Yes. I, along with Sheriff Lieutenant Al D'Urso of Rockingham County, located one safety deposit box belonging to Mr. Anderson at Fleet Bank on North Broadway in Salem, NH."

"Did you find any other safety deposit boxes belonging to Mr. Anderson?"

"No, that was the only one."

"Can you tell the court what you found?"

"It contained nearly $270,000 in cash and securities. There was a passbook for a savings account that contained $54,000, there was $38,000 in cash in one hundred dollar bills, there were seven CD's, certificates of deposit, totaling $135,000 and six treasury bonds totaling $42,700. One of the treasury bonds was made out to both Robert Anderson and Pam McEvoy and it was for $10,000."

"Detective Rheault, was this safety deposit box in only Robert Anderson's name?"

"Yes."

"So Amy Anderson's name wasn't on it?"

"That's correct."

"Did you have a chance to talk to Mr. Anderson's family concerning the safety deposit box?"

"Yes. I spoke to his mother in law, his parents, who were up here from Florida, his brother and sister in law, who moved into the Anderson house, and Robert's siblings. No one in his family knew anything about the money, securities or safety deposit box."

"Did you talk to Ms. McEvoy?

"Yes, she was aware of the $10,000 treasury bond made out to her and Mr. Anderson. She informed me that Robert told her that he had one made out to her and him. She told me that she would get it if the business had a good year. Ms. McEvoy was also the person who told me about the possible existence of the safety deposit box."

"After you located the safety deposit box and its contents, was Attorney Carpenito made aware of its contents."

"The family gave me permission to speak to Attorney Carpenito and I made him aware of its contents."

"And are you aware of his subsequent actions?"

"Yes. He attached the assets pending a wrongful death lawsuit brought forth by the co-guardians of the children, Amy Anderson's mother and sister."

"Thank you detective, no further questions."

****

Attorney Carney then approached detective Rheault.

"Detective, did you have any interaction with the Anderson family prior to the murder of Amy Anderson?"

"Yes. I would see Amy's mother usually once a week. She worked at Daisy Cleaners with one of my sisters."

"Did you have much interaction with Amy Anderson?"

"Only on occasions."

"So you had no way of knowing whether she had knowledge of the safety deposit box?"

"That's correct."

"So, she could have known about the safety deposit box."

"That's possible."

"No further questions your honor."

****

Judge Barton adjourned court for the day and week. It would resume on Monday and there would be no testimony on Friday. The reason for this was believed to be one of the juror's child was getting married on Friday.

****

The following day, Friday, the Eagle Tribune covered the case and reporter Bill Murphy gave a synopsis of the courts preceding's under the headline: "Defense paints Anderson as pathetic and lovestruck."

****

June 19, 1995
Monday

Morgan Dexter was the lab technician from the Mass State Police lab who testified concerning the ceiling tile dust and blood splatters found on Robert Anderson's jacket from the night of the murder. Her testimony first centered around the blood splatter on Robert Anderson's jacket that could only have occurred as a result of a blunt force instrument.

Prosecutor McAlary began by asking Dexter to explain the composition of blood and different types of blood splatters.

Dexter stated that blood is actually an organ that is composed primarily of plasma and red blood cells. Plasma is a liquid that contains protein in suspension. Red blood cells carry oxygen. When blood leaves the body, it coagulates quickly and becomes a solid quickly and transfers to other surfaces, particularly clothes.

Mrs. Dexter then went on to explain that this blood transfer to clothes can result in three different types of stains: a passive stain occurs when indirect forces, such as gravity, cause the blood to be drops or pools. Dexter further explained that "This type of stain is circular in nature with radials emanating out from it like rays of the sun."

"The next type is a transfer stain. This occurs when surrounding objects, such as clothes, come in contact with the blood of a victim. They can be drag marks, fingerprints, or shoe prints etcetera."

Dexter continued, "The last type of stain is a projected impact stain. These occur by blood that travels in the air. It is generally the result of some force that is exerted on the body. They are somewhat circular in shape with a blood tail at the end."

"Why is that Mrs. Dexter?" McAlary asked.

"It's a result of inertia, one of Newton's laws of motion. There is an equal and opposite reaction for every action."

"Mrs. Dexter let me try and simplify this for the jury. If I stood to your side and gave you a vicious blow with a five pound steel blunt instrument, like a wrench, that penetrated your skin and skull, would there be blood splatter that would come back onto me."

"Yes, there would be."

McAlary then walked to the prosecutors table and grabbed a jacket and showed it to Dexter.

"Mrs. Dexter, do you recognize this jacket."

"Yes I do, this was the jacket brought to me at the state lab by Trooper Zuk and identified to me by Trooper Zuk as belonging to Robert Anderson. It is the jacket he wore the night of the murder of Amy Anderson."

"And is this the jacket you examined?"

"Yes it is. I recognize the jacket as the one I examined and I left a State Lab tag indicating the date I received it, the date I examined it, and my name."

"Mrs. Dexter please tell the court your findings."

"Yes. The blood on the jacket was that of Amy Anderson."

"How were you able to ascertain that?"

"By DNA analysis which was performed by the State Lab Chemist."

"Were there blood splatters on the jacket?"

"Yes. There were two types, transfer stains and impact stains."

"Mrs. Dexter, you heard Patrolman Waller's testimony on how Mr. Anderson cradled his wife's head."

"Yes."

"Would this cause blood splatter and what type?"

"Yes it would and it would be a passive stain. There were smudges and stains on the jacket."

"And what was the other type of splatter?"

"It was impact splatter."

Prosecutor Mc Alary walked to the prosecutors table and once again grabbed the blood stained five pound wrench.

"Mrs. Dexter, do you recognize this wrench."

"Yes I do. That was also delivered to me by Trooper Zuk. I subsequently examined that and found it to have blood and brown hair imbedded in it."

"Did you also do a DNA analysis on this?"

"Yes I did. It was the blood and hair of Amy Anderson."

"Any doubt."

"None whatsoever."

"And could the impact splatters on Robert Anderson's jacket have been caused by him striking Amy Anderson repeatedly in the head?"

"Yes it would, and since there were splatters up and down the right arm and on the shoulders of the jacket, they would have been strong blows because in blunt force injuries, such as beatings and hitting, the objects have a wider surface and thus more blood will be deposited on the object resulting in varying sizes of the droplets. This was the case on the jacket I examined."

"Were you able to ascertain how many times Amy Anderson was hit."

"Yes, at least four times and it appeared that it was from the driver's side of the van."

"Mrs. Dexter, besides blood, did you find anything else on Mr. Anderson's jacket?"

"Yes, I found dust that I was able to link to the ceiling tiles that were found in the Cherry and Webb building next to the Shawmut bank. They matched the dust on Mr. Anderson's jacket."

"Can you please be more specific?"

"The dust contained asbestos. To be more exact, amosite asbestos. This was in ceiling tiles prior to 1976. The ceiling tiles in Cherry and Webb's contained amosite asbestos where the murder weapon and other objects were found.

"Thank you. No further questions your honor."

****

"Mrs. Dexter, you said that a number of different things can cause an impact splatter," attorney Carney said as he began his cross-examination.

"Yes."

"If Mr. Anderson saw his wife in the van and grabbed her and went to hold her…" as Carney was saying this he held out his two hands and arms and quickly pulled them in, "Would this cause impact splatter."

"It could, but not to the degree I examined on Mr. Andersons jacket."

"But that could cause impact splatter if a loving husband did that and held his beaten wife to his chest."

"Yes."

"Thank you."

"Mrs. Dexter, could the blood splatter on Mr. Anderson's clothes also be caused by Mrs. Anderson gagging on blood and spitting up on Mr. Anderson's clothes?"

"Spit-up blood can cause splatter, but I don't think that was what caused the splatter on Mr. Anderson's clothes because of the breath of the splatter."

"Mrs. Dexter, I'd like to now address the ceiling tile dust on Robert Anderson's jacket. Where you aware that Mr. Anderson and his wife had been working above ceiling tiles in a South Lawrence Bank before he and his wife met the other two cleaners at Shawmut bank?"

"I was not made aware that Mr. Anderson had been working above ceiling tiles in another bank."

"So you didn't test any other tiles?"

"That is correct."

"That will be all."

Judge Barton looked towards the prosecution table, "Have you anything on redirect."

"Yes your honor."

"Mrs. Dexter, the blood splatter that you examined on the defendants jacket, would it be more indicative of multiple vicious blows to the head, or grabbing someone quickly and holding them to you."

"It would be the former, multiple vicious blows to the head."

"And you said there were at least four blows to the head"

"Yes."

"Thank You."

Authors note: It was never determined if Robert and Amy Anderson had been at another bank in South Lawrence prior to coming to the Shawmut Bank which is in North Lawrence. It appears unlikely given the timeline from when the Andersons left their home on Golden Oaks in Salem, NH.

****

The previous week in the OJ Simpson trial, blood evidence was introduced that unequivocally showed OJ

Simpson's blood was found at the murder scene of Ron Goldman and Nicole Brown Simpson. Like Mrs. Dexter, there was testimony that the chances of that not being OJ Simpsons blood was over one-billion to one. It appears that during jury deliberations, this was not an important factor considered by the Simpson jury.

****

The next witness was Rebecca O'Brien who hired Robert Anderson's company to do work at her home after experiencing water damage in January of 1994.

"Mrs. O'Brien, did you have occasion to call a ServiceMaster franchise owned by Robert Anderson on January 20th of last year?"

"Yes, we had a burst pipe on Thursday, January 20th, of last year and the plumber who fixed the pipe recommended a ServiceMaster owned by Mr. Anderson for the cleanup."

"Did you call this ServiceMaster?"

"Yes I did and the receptionist, or maybe the answering service, told me that the owner, Mr. Anderson, would get back to me within the hour."

"Did that happen?"

"Yes in about thirty minutes. Mr. Anderson emphasized to me that the remediation should happen quickly to avoid more damage or the possibility of mold developing."

"What happened next?"

"I told him I would talk to my husband, which I did."

"And then what happened?"

"I called Mr. Anderson later that night and asked when he could come over and he said tomorrow, so we hired him."

"Did he have a crew come over the next day?"

"Yes, and they did a good job."

"What did they do?

They cleaned all the rugs except the one in the bedroom that had extensive damage. They cut out half the carpet. In addition, they also took some sheetrock out that had gotten soaked from the broken pipe and the insulation behind it. They also put heaters, dehumidifiers and fans throughout the house to dry everything out."

"When did they take this equipment out?"

"Monday morning, the 24th I believe."

"When did you and your husband move back into the house?"

"After the crew left Monday morning. My husband met them and unlocked the house for them so they could get their heaters and fans. He then came back to our friend's house and we got all our belongings, and moved back into our house."

"And did Mr. Anderson have occasion to come into your house?"

"Yes he did. He came that Monday afternoon to inspect the crews work."

"And what happened?"

"He came in the late afternoon and I showed him where the work was done. He seemed to know what he was doing because he took pictures of all the work his crew had done. One of the members of the crew had taken 'before' pictures prior to them beginning the remediation the previous Friday. Mr. Anderson said that he would take care of everything with the insurance company and if there were any problems to call him."

"Were you with Mr. Anderson all the time?"

"No I wasn't. There was about 10 minutes when he was alone and I was in the kitchen."

"Did you notice anything missing after he left."

"Yes. Later that night my husband noticed that his 9 mm handgun was missing."

"And where was it before it went missing."

"It was on the bureau in our bedroom."

"And by our bedroom you mean you and your husband?"

"Yes."

"And after noticing the gun was missing, did you call the police?"

"Yes we did, but not until the next day. My husband wanted to make sure that he didn't misplace it."

"After you called the police, what happened?"

"A cruiser came by and the officer took a report. We had all the paperwork for the gun so I gave him the make, model and serial number."

"Were you eventually contacted concerning the gun being recovered?"

"Yes I was, during the first week in March of last year. I was contacted by the Manchester police. They told me that they were contacted by Lawrence, Mass police and that the gun may have been used in a murder or was part of a murder investigation."

Prosecutor McAlary walked to the prosecution table and took a gun from the table. It was an automatic 9 mm, with the slide back that had a trigger lock and a slide lock. It was evident to all that it was unloaded. Nonetheless, he showed it to one of the court Sheriffs who confirmed it was unloaded.

"Mrs. McAlary as you can see the gun is not loaded and there is no magazine in it. Can you confirm this to the court?"

"Yes I can. It is not loaded and even if it wasn't, it wouldn't be able to shoot because of the two locks. I shoot and I'm comfortable around guns"

"Thank you. Can you confirm to the court that this is the gun that you reported stolen from your home after Mr. Anderson left?"

"May I see it please?" and as she said this she looked at some paperwork that she took out of her handbag.

"Yes it is my gun."

"How can you tell?"

"Well, I can tell that it's the same make and model by looking at it, and I have the gun's paperwork here, including the bill of sale that has the gun's serial number, and it matches."

"Mrs. O'Brien, the defense has insinuated that this gun may have been stolen the day the remediation crew was in your house, Friday, January 21st. Is that possible?"

"No, it's impossible. The pipes burst on the Thursday before the crew was there. We moved out of our house that Thursday after the plumber fixed the pipes. We went to a friend's house and I brought the gun with us in a lock box to that friend's house. The Monday we moved back was when the gun was back in the house and this was after the remediation crew left."

"So just to recap, the gun that you reported stolen was not in the house from Thursday night until Monday afternoon after the crew left and before Mr. Anderson arrived?"

"That's correct."

Mrs. O'Brien, did you have any other visitors that day or night.

"No we did not."

"Do you always lock your doors?"

"Always."

"Thank you. No further questions."

****

Jay Carney got slowly out of his seat and walked towards the witness stand while checking his notes.

"Mrs. O'Brien, you said that you didn't report the missing handgun right away because you and your husband wanted to make sure you didn't misplace it. Is that correct?"

"Yes, but I'm reasonably certain that the gun was left on the bureau."

"But not 100% certain, because you didn't call the police right away."

"We didn't call the police right away, just so we could double check."

"Thank you. So did you check around the house?"

"Yes."

"Did you check the car?"

"Yes we did. But just to make sure."

"So if it was left in the car, someone could have stolen it from the car."

"We always lock the car."

"But thieves can get into a locked car can't they.

"I'm sure it's happened."

"Thank you. No further questions."

****

McAlary was brief on redirect.

"Mrs. O'Brien, where was your car parked on the Monday you came home?"

"It was in the garage."

"Was the car locked?"

"Yes it was. I always lock the car, even in the garage. I had a theft from my car once when it wasn't unlocked. Since then I've been in the habit of always locking it, even in the garage."

"How about your husband's car."

"Same."

"Is your garage locked?"

"Always, and we have a garage door opener and always close the door since there is a door in the garage leading into our house."

"So when the door is down, it is in fact locked."

"Yes."

"After the gun was stolen, were there any signs of forced entry into your house or garage."

"No."

"Thank you. No further questions."

Judge Barton adjourned court for the day.

****

After court was adjourned, Attorney McAlary spoke to members of the press where he stated he believed that Anderson was buried by the testimony of the trio of women, specifically, Pam McEvoy, Morgan Dexter and Rebecca O'Brien. McAlary went on to elaborate how the testimony of each of the woman pointed the finger at Anderson and no one else. He also felt that their testimony was an exoneration of William Prince.

****

June 20, 1995
Tuesday

The first witness of the day was Detective Jack McDonald of Lawrence police department.

"Detective McDonald, did you take part in the Amy Anderson murder investigation?"

"Yes. I received a call from Captain Mollohan, on the night she was murdered. The murder, I believe, was reported at 7 PM, and I received a call about an hour after that."

"Did you head up the investigation?"

"Yes, I along with Trooper Norman Zuk of the Mass State Police. We've worked together a number of times in the past on murder investigations and work well together."

"Did you have a suspect?"

"Yes. We suspected Amy's husband, Robert Anderson, right from the beginning."

"Thank you. I'd like to draw your attention to March 2, the Wednesday after the murder. Did you receive a phone call that morning?"

"Yes. I received a phone call from the manager of the Shawmut bank in Lawrence, Judith Smith."

"And what was the gist of the call."

"She told me she was following the Anderson murder in the papers and even though we, the police, didn't give any indication of any suspects, she said she figured we were looking at Robert Anderson. She then went on to say that her facilities director had given Robert Anderson the key to the vacant Cherry and Webb building and had never gotten it back."

"What happened then?"

"I asked her how many times he had gone in there and why. She told me that he said there was a dust problem caused by the boiler and he wanted to check it out, that's when we gave him the key for the first time."

"For the first time?"

"Yes, the manager then told me that after Mr. Anderson came out and gave her facilities person the key back, Mr. Anderson said he forgot a tool in the building, was given the key, and never gave it back after he went in."

"Please continue detective."

"I then asked her if she had another key to get in the building and she said she did. I asked her if we could get the key and check the building. At this time, we hadn't found the murder weapons and we thought maybe they were in the Cherry and Webb building. Prior to going in the building we also received permission from her to search the building.

"After you got the key, what happened?"

"We went in the building, which had electricity, and went right to the boiler room."

"Who was with you?"

"My partner Mike Laird, Trooper Norman Zuk and Lieutenant Milone of State Police,"

"Did you find anything?"

"Yes we did."

"Can you please describe what you found?"

"The first room we entered was the boiler room because that was the room that Mr. Anderson supposedly went into. We searched the room and closets and didn't find anything. That's when I looked up and saw that one of the ceiling tiles wasn't sitting right after we noticed a stain on the floor under it. We couldn't reach the tiles because the ceilings were twelve feet high. This was when my partner, Mike Laird, remembered seeing a ladder in a closet in the boiler room. He got the ladder, and he went up it to push the ceiling tile out of the way. That's when we found the three tools that were subsequently identified as the murder weapons. They were in a bag on top of an adjacent tile."

"Did you find anything else?"

"Yes, we found two handguns, a 9 mm and a .25-caliber and a pair of bloody gloves. They were also in the same bag with the murder weapons."

"What happened next?"

Detective McDonald then went on to describe how the murder weapons and two guns were rushed to the state lab in Salem, Ma after a forensic team from State Police was called. At the lab it was determined that that the 9 mm handgun was stolen and quite possibly the .25-caliber too. The lab also found Robert Anderson's fingerprint on the .25-caliber and the blood on the wrench, carpet cutter and phillips screwdriver was the same type as Amy Anderson's. DNA testing would take another three to five days."

"What did you do about the guns?"

"After we ran the serial numbers on the guns, we determined who the owners were and contacted them. The owner of the .25-caliber was a Wendy Jack of Derry, NH. When I contacted her, she advised me that the gun belonged to her father who lived with her and her husband. After her father died, she knew that it was in the top draw of his bureau, but had forgotten about it until I called. When I asked her if she knew Mr. Anderson, she told me they had been long-time friends."

"Detective McDonald, what did you do next?"

"With all the other evidence we obtained, we felt we had sufficient probable cause for an arrest warrant. We obtained the warrant, went to Salem, NH PD where we spoke to Detective Fred Rheault and Lieutenant Richard Dunn. Salem Detectives then obtained a fugitive from justice warrant for Robert Anderson."

"And when did you place him under arrest."

"By that time, the wake for Amy was underway and there was a tremendous amount of people waiting to pay their respects. We decided to wait until after the wake to arrest him. He was arrested at 9:30 PM. The warrant was effected by Detective Rheault and Detective Phillips. He was then taken to the station and booked, and was brought to court the next morning where his attorney waived extradition."

"Thank you detective. No further questions."

****

Attorney Carney asked his first question.

"Detective McDonald, were there any witnesses to the murder of Amy Anderson?"

"No sir."

"Were there any witnesses that saw anyone go into the Cherry and Webb building the evening of the murder?"

"No sir."

"You said that you found the murder weapons in the ceiling tiles of the boiler room in the Cherry and Webb building. Is that correct?"

"Yes it is."

"And you also said that you needed a ladder to reach the ceiling tiles where the murder weapons were concealed?"

"Yes sir."

"So does it stand to reason that the murderer would have needed that ladder?"

"Yes sir."

"Was the ladder ever fingerprinted?"

"Yes, but we found no usable prints."

"Thank you."

McAlary had one question on redirect.

"Detective McDonald, what evidence do you have linking Robert Anderson to the murder weapons found in the ceiling tiles?"

"To re-iterate, Robert Anderson's fingerprint on the .25-caliber weapon in his possession that was found with the murder weapons in addition to the bloody Cherry and Webb key that was found in his house. We also found matching gloves and trash bags at his business similar to the ones in the ceiling."

"Thank you."

****

For his next witness, prosecutor McAlary called Wendy Jack to the stand.

Mrs. Jack stated that she was an assistant school superintendent in Manchester, NH and she and her husband had been friends with the Anderson's since the mid-seventies.

"Mrs. Jack, how did you know the Anderson's?"

"I first met Amy Anderson in 1975 when we were both teaching English at Salem, NH high school. We became close friends and socialized two or three times a month since then."

"Mrs. Jack, you heard Detective McDonald's testimony. Were you familiar with the .25-caliber gun he was referring too?"

"Yes I was. My dad had been living with us for about ten years before he died in 1991, and I knew he had that gun. After he died, I had forgotten all about it."

Did Mr. Anderson have access to your house when you were away for whatever reason?"

"Yes he did. As I said, we were long-time friends with the Anderson's and I gave Robert a key to check the house when we were away, especially in the winter when we went on vacation. My husband and I always worried about frozen pipes."

"And did Mr. Anderson check your house when you were away on vacation?"

"Yes, numerous times, and he would always call us and let us know everything was alright."

"So he could have taken the gun that belonged to your father, especially since his fingerprint was on it."

"Yes, it's possible."

"Thank you Mrs. Jack, no further questions."

Jay Carney approached the witness stand.

"Mrs. Jack, you stated that you never noticed the gun was missing. Is that correct."

"Yes it is."

"Could there be other items around the house that are missing, but you haven't noticed it yet."

After a moment's hesitation, "Yes, that is possible."

"Mrs. Jack, do you keep a house key hidden outside your house in the event you get locked out? And please, you don't have to reveal the location."

"Yes we do."

"So isn't it possible, that someone could have found the key, entered your house, and taken an item or two that you're not aware of and put the key back, including the .25-caliber gun?"

"Yes, it's possible."

"Is it also possible that your father gave the gun away?"

"Yes, it's possible."

"No further questions."

Fred McAlary stood up from the prosecutor's table and said, "Your honor, I'd like to recall Detective McDonald as a rebuttal to Mr. Carney's line of questioning. I just have a one question."

"That's fine."

Jack McDonald was called back to the witness stand.

"Detective McDonald, you realize you're still under oath."

"Yes sir I do."

"Detective, were there any other fingerprints on the .25-caliber gun in question besides the defendants?"

"No sir. That was the only one."

"Thank you."

"Attorney Carney rose to his feet."

"Detective, were there any fingerprints on the 9 mm gun that was found."

"There was a smudge, but not usable."

"No doubt, the gun was handled prior to you finding it."

"No doubt."

"Therefore, isn't it possible that someone else could have handled the .25-caliber gun and not left fingerprints, especially if they wore gloves?"

"It's possible."

"No further questions."

Prosecutor McAlary rose from his table.

"Just a couple of questions on redirect your honor."

"Go ahead," Judge Barton replied.

"Detective, was the defendant's fingerprint on the .25-caliber smudged at all?"

"No it wasn't, it was very clear."

"If someone handled the gun wearing gloves, would the fingerprint have been smudged?"

"Most likely."

"Thank you."

Prosecutor McAlary returned to his table and Detective McDonald stepped down.

"Your next witness Attorney McAlary."

"Your honor, the state rests."

Judge Barton then looked towards Attorney Carney and gestured.

"Your honor, the state is only going to call one witness, Robert Anderson, the defendant. However, I would like to first make a motion."

"Go ahead with your motion counselor."

"Your honor, the defense would like to make a motion to dismiss all charges against the defendant since the prosecution has failed to prove its case."

"The basis for your motion?" Judge Barton asked.

"Your honor, Robert was in fact at Shawmut Bank the night Amy Anderson was murdered, but the state has produced no witnesses as to who committed the murder. Mr. Anderson cannot be linked to the murder weapons except through the two guns in the bag, and Robert's employee, Mr. Prince had access to both guns. The government's case is built on speculation and surmise. Essentially your honor, it is smoke and mirrors based on circumstantial evidence alone."

In his rebuttal to Attorney Carney, Prosecutor McAlary stated, "No matter how you twist the evidence in this case, it points to the defendant and the defendant alone, and no one else. The evidence in the bag points solidly to Mr. Anderson. Everything in that bag in addition to the blood evidence and witness testimony points to the Defendant."

After a moment's contemplation, Judge Barton stated he is going to dismiss court for the day and rule on the motion at the beginning of court tomorrow.

"Attorney Carney, be prepared to call your witness tomorrow in the event I rule against your motion."

"Yes your honor."

****

Outside the courtroom, Fred McAlary said to reporters that he wasn't surprised over the defense's motion since that happens in most murder trials, and he is confident that Judge Barton will deny the motion, and the jury will subsequently find the defendant guilty."

When attorney Carney was asked about putting Anderson on the stand, he stated, "I think the strongest evidence I have in this case is for Bob Anderson to take the stand and look the jurors in the eyes and say, 'I did not do this.' Robert Anderson will be his own best witness."
Author's note: The Anderson children did not have to testify since the prosecution had previously stipulated that Robert and Amy never argued in front of them.

****

June 21, 1995
Wednesday

At 9 AM, after he was seated, Judge Barton, to no surprise, denied the motion to dismiss the charges against the defendant and Attorney Carney called Robert Anderson to the stand. To say the courtroom was packed would have been an understatement and a number of observers were barred entry because of fire code regulations. They were directed to another courtroom where a closed circuit television was set up so they could observe the proceedings.

After being sworn in and identifying himself, attorney Carney wasted no time getting to the heart of the matter,

"Did you ever say to Pam McEvoy that you would never leave Amy?"

"Yes I did. I told her that she was the best mother and wife a husband could have. She wasn't only the best wife and mother, she was my best friend."

"Did you ever kiss Ms. McEvoy?"

"No I did not."

"Did you ever tell her you loved her?"

"Never," Anderson said with emphasis."

"Did you ever have any type of sexual relations with her?"

"Never," also with emphasis.

"When did you hire Ms. McEvoy?"

"I hired her in October of 1993."

"Why did you hire her?"

"I was working 65 to 70 hours a week and I wanted to free up more of my time so I could spend it with my wife and children."

"Once she was hired, how did you train her and what were her responsibilities?"

"Driving around alone for over 60 hours per week is tough. She did travel with me a lot and we went from client to client."

"Did you become friendly with her?

"Yes. We got along well and when you're spending that much time together, you get friendly, and it was great to have someone to talk to."

"Describe your relationship with Ms. McEvoy please."

"It was very friendly but platonic. I met her while cleaning her parent's apartment. She was living with them and her young son. She was a struggling single parent selling cosmetics at a retail outlet. She was friendly and personable and I thought she would be a good fit as a marketing specialist. I was also trying to help her out."

"Besides her pay, did you give Ms. McEvoy any money after she was initially hired?"

"Yes, I noticed that during the first couple of weeks she worked for me, she wore the same clothes a lot. She told me that she couldn't afford to buy a lot of clothes, so I gave her $100 to buy clothes for the job."

"Did you ever tell her to dress in a sexually suggestive manner?"

"Never. I told her that business casual was good. I never told any female employee that."

Up until this time, whenever Robert Anderson answered a question, he looked directly at the jury. However, after he answered the last question, he noticed prosecutor McAlary whisper something to his assistant who left the courtroom. Anderson temporarily took his eyes off the jury to observe the exchange. His attention was brought back by attorney Carney and his next question.

"Mr. Anderson, did you ever give Ms. McEvoy any gifts?"

"Yes, I gave her flowers on Valentine's Day, and when she told me her son's TV broke and she couldn't afford to buy him a new one, I bought a TV for her son."

"You heard testimony from Ms. McEvoy that during the twenty-four days before Christmas, you gave her a gift every day. Is that true?"

"No it isn't. I gave her a couple of gifts for Christmas including a Teddy Bear for her son but definitely not a gift every day, and some of the gifts she mentioned I did in fact get, but they went to other employees."

"Did you take her out to lunch every day?"

"I noticed the first couple of days Ms. McEvoy worked with me she brought a brown bag lunch and it wasn't much, so I told her I'd spring for lunch on the days she worked. Sometimes it was just a drive through at a fast food joint."

"Did you take her out at any other time?"

"At one point she told me that she liked the ballet but could never afford it. So as a Christmas bonus I took her to the ballet preceded by dinner."

"What did you do after the ballet?"

"I took her right home."

"And to re-iterate, you never had any kind of sex with her?"

"Never."

Attorney Carney paused for a moment while consulting his notes.

"Robert, I know this is going to be difficult, but I'd like to turn your attention to the night of your wife's murder"

"Yes," Anderson said with downcast eyes.

"Please explain what happened the night she was murdered, beginning with you and her leaving the house."

Anderson testified that he had asked his wife to help him that evening because it was a Saturday night and by her helping, his other two workers could get home early. They left the house late afternoon and before going to the Shawmut bank, they went to another client, a bank in south Lawrence to check the work of some other workers.

After arriving at the Shawmut bank, his two workers were waiting for them and they all carried cleaning supplies into the building.

"Robert, did you tell William Prince and Tracy Enzo not to use the stairwell leading to the basement because the door was locked and alarmed?" attorney Carney asked.

"No I did not."

Anderson then recounted how he asked Amy to go out for refreshments for the cleaning crew. After walking her to the corner to try and find a nearby open convenience store, he walked her to the van because he was concerned about her safety since Lawrence was noted for its violence.

"I told her it wasn't a good place to walk and told her to take the van," Anderson stated.

"What happened then?"

"I went back into the bank and Ms. Enzo and I began cleaning upstairs while Mr. Prince remained alone in the basement cleaning."

"Did Ms. Enzo point out what she thought was a blood stain on your sweatshirt?"

"She pointed out a stain, not a blood stain. She asked if I spilled anything. I went into the bathroom and washed it off. I told her afterwards it looked like a dirty water stain that could've happened when I was moving the mop buckets."

"Please continue."

"After about twenty to thirty minutes, I saw the van's taillights after I looked out the door, and assumed my wife had returned. I told Tracy I was going out to help her. When I got to the van, the driver's side door was open and I saw Amy slumped over towards the passenger's seat. I thought she was getting something on the floor. When I got closer, there was blood all over the place. She was gurgling, she was trying to say something." While saying this, Anderson's voice began to crack and there were tears in his eyes. Before he asked his next question, attorney Carney paused while Anderson appeared to compose himself.

"What did you do then?"

"I knew she needed help. I ran to the bank and began pounding on the door and screaming to Tracy to call the police, I said 'someone please call 911, someone beat my wife.' She couldn't get an outside line so I did it. I then ran back to the van."

"Please go on."

"When I got back to the van, I went in the passenger's side and I cradled Amy's head in my arms. I was talking to her and telling her she would be alright. The police and ambulance arrived a short time later, and I went with her in the ambulance to the hospital."

"Did you have blood on you?"

"Yes. My jacket was covered with Amy's blood from me holding her and spitting up on me," Anderson said. His voice once again cracked and his eyes teared.

"Thank you."

Judge Barton, at this point, called for a brief ten minute recess. He had noticed that some of the jurors were crying and upset.

****

"Mr. Anderson, I'd like to now turn your attention to Mr. William Prince. When did you hire him?"

"I hired him in 1989, not long after he got out of the marines. He had been on the gymnastic team I coached when I was the Athletic Director at Salem, High. He was also in a couple of my phys ed classes."

"Was he a good employee?"

"Yes. He was a good worker but I always felt something was wrong. I sometimes got the feeling he may have been jealous and I caught him looking at Amy a lot."

"Did he have a lot of responsibility?"

"Yes, like I said he was a good employee."

"Did you ever give him the key to the Cherry and Webb building?"

"Yes I did."

"When?"

"On the night Amy was murdered. I gave it to him shortly after we arrived at the Shawmut bank."

"Why did you do this?"

"I was trying to win the contract to do ventilation work in the Cherry and Webb building and Mr. Prince excelled at this. I told him at some point to go and check it out."

"Whatever happened to the key? Did Mr. Prince ever give it back to you?"

"No, he never gave me the key back, and with what happened to Amy, there were more important things on my mind."

"Did Mr. Prince come to your home after the murder?"

"Yes, I believe it was the Monday before the first day of the wake. The entire family was over and we were reminiscing about Amy and caring for my two daughters. Mr. Prince came in to pay his respects and we invited him into the house."

"Did he stay long?"

"I'm not sure because people were coming and going. But I remember taking his coat and him staying for some food and drink that we had."

"Where were most people at this time?"

"Mainly in the dining and living room."

"And where was Mr. Prince?"

"He mingled but I remembered seeing him in the kitchen when there was no one there. I figured that he was getting something to eat or drink."

"And where was the key to Cherry and Webb found."

"I was told my sister-in-law found it in the kitchen on top of one of the cabinets."

"So someone, who was alone in the kitchen, could have put that key up there with no one noticing."

"Yes."

"Thank you. You heard the testimony of Mrs. Jack concerning her Dad's .25-caliber handgun?"

"Yes I did."

"And Mrs. Jack said you were friendly with her and her family?"

"That's correct. Amy and I met them in 1975 when we were student teaching and we've been friends ever since."

"The prosecution inferred from Mrs. Jacks testimony that while you had access to her house you stole her father's .25-caliber gun."

"That couldn't be further from the truth. He and I were talking one day on how I had a lot of clients in Lawrence and I was always worried about the random violence in Lawrence. He then asked me if I wanted the gun. He said that he didn't want it around the house anymore because he was getting old and he didn't want to take the chance of the grandkids getting it. I told him that I would take it since it was easily concealable."

"Where did you keep this gun?"

"I kept it in the van in a little storage compartment behind the front seat."

"Was Mr. Prince aware of this?"

"Yes he was."

"Did he have access to the gun?"

"Yes, he could have gotten it anytime."

"When was the last time you saw the gun?"

"About two weeks before Amy was murdered."

"And did you notice the gun was missing?"

"No I didn't. If I did, I would have reported it to the police."

"Thank you. No further questions."

Before Prosecutor McAlary began his cross examination, Judge Barton adjourned court for lunch.

****

After lunch, McAlary began his cross-examination of Anderson.

"Mr. Anderson, you said you gave Pam McEvoy $100 to buy clothes?"

"Yes I did."

"And you also said that you took her to the ballet and dinner?"

"Yes."

"And is it true that you got her flowers on Valentine's Day and bought her a TV and bought her lunch almost every day while working."

"Yes. As I said, the TV was for her son."

"So isn't it safe to say that Pam McEvoy was a special type of employee."

"No, she was an employee. I treated them pretty much the same."

"If that's the case Mr. Anderson, what other employee did you buy lunch for every day they worked with you, bought them flowers and a TV, and took to the ballet and dinner at posh Boston restaurants?

"I bought other employees gifts like I previously testified and I would go out drinking with them and buy drinks sometimes after work."

"And you previously testified that you never told Ms. McEvoy to dress sexy for clients or any other employee for that matter. Is that correct?"

"Yes it is."

"Did you set up a trust fund for Ms. McEvoy as she testified?"

"No I did not."

"Did you ever seek a sexual relationship with Ms. McEvoy which she resisted?"

"No I did not. I never made any advances to her or any other employee, so there was nothing to resist."

McAlary briefly looked at his notes before continuing.

"Did you take Ms. McEvoy to dinner at Anthony's Pier 4 and a Garth Brooks concert eight days before your wife was brutally murdered."

Anderson hesitated momentarily before answering.

"Yes I did."

"Did your wife Amy know that you took Pam McEvoy to the ballet, Garth Brooks and dinner?"

"Yes she did."

"And she wasn't the least bit concerned?"

"That's correct. I told Amy everything and she wasn't concerned because I told her that Ms. McEvoy was just an employee and I felt bad for her because of her life situation."

"So you're telling this court that your wife, Amy, was not the least bit concerned over this relationship?"

"My wife had asked me if I was having an affair with Ms. McEvoy but she said this as a prelude to a joke. Amy joked that she would be surprised that anyone would be interested in me."

Once again, McAlary consulted his notes.

"Mr. Anderson, did your wife consider taking a leave of absence from her teaching duties at Salem High in January of 1994 because she was upset with your relationship with Pam McEvoy and the state of your marriage?"

"I had never heard Amy say that."

"So you weren't concerned that your wife would divorce you and you would have to subsequently have to divide your wealth? You stood a great deal to lose"

"No, not at all. Amy and I had a good marriage and divorce was not an issue. Even if it was, I would have no trouble splitting the wealth. I would want to provide for Amy and my daughters."

"Mr. Anderson, did you have a safety deposit box with over two-hundred thousand in cash and liquid securities?"

"Yes I did."

"Was your wife aware of this?"

"I believe so. We had no secrets."

"And was your wife also aware that one of the CD's was in both your name and Ms. McEvoy's name?"

"Yes I believe so."

"You believe so?"

"Yes."

"Mr. Anderson, on the night of your wife's murder, you sent her out for drinks. Is that correct?"

"Yes."

"Why did you do this when there was a Pepsi and snack machine in the basement of the bank you were cleaning?"

Once again Anderson hesitated before answering.

"I guess I forgot."

"Too bad. Because if you didn't, your wife would've been alive today, or would she?"

Attorney Carney immediately objected to the question.

"That's okay you're Honor, I withdraw the question," McAlary responded.

For the next hour McAlary grilled Anderson. Specifically on how his testimony differed from all other prosecution witnesses, especially Tracy Enzo and William Prince. For the most part, Anderson kept his composure though there were some lapses in his memory.

"One last question Mr. Anderson, if we are to believe your testimony today, doesn't it mean that every other witness was lying?"

Once again attorney Carney objected and once again, Prosecutor McAlary withdrew the question; but not before, he felt, that he had indelibly printed the seeds of doubt in the mind of the jurors.

Robert Anderson was on the witness stand for over five hours.

****

Attorney Carney had no questions on redirect and rested his case. Prosecutor McAlary then requested to call Francesca Lopez as a rebuttal witness.

Attorney Carney immediately objected and asked to approach the bench. Judge Barton adjourned court for a recess and asked both attorneys to join him in his chambers.

Once in his chambers, Judge Barton began.

"I believe I know what your objection is Mr. Carney.

"Yes your honor. You had previously ruled that the jury would not hear any testimony on any previous sexual assault allegations against my client."

"Yes I did. Mr. McAlary, your response.

"Your honor, Mr. Carney and Mr. Anderson opened the door. Mr. Anderson testified that he never told Ms. McEvoy to dress sexy and he also testified that he never came on to Ms. McEvoy or any other employee. Ms. Lopez's testimony will directly contradict this."

Before Attorney Carney responded, Judge Barton spoke.

"Attorney Carney, I know you're not going to be happy. But I'm going to allow her testimony. As Prosecutor McAlary stated, you opened the door."

Attorney Carney wisely, just nodded.

Fred McAlary thought to himself that even though Carney opened the door, he's going to slam it shut.

****

Once court resumed, McAlary called Francesca Lopez to the stand. After identifying herself, McAlary started his questioning.

"Ms. Lopez did you ever work for Mr. Anderson?"

"Yes I did, briefly."

"How did this come about?"

"His company did some cleaning at my parent's Methuen home in January of 1994 after we had water damage. He came twice to the house and after the second time, he offered me a job."

"What was this job?"

"He said I would be a marketing assistant."

"How old were you at the time?"

"I was eighteen."

"Did you have any experience in this field or take any courses in marketing?"

"No, none at all."

"Did he describe to you the requirements of the job?"

"Yes he did. He told me I could get a taste of the job right after he was done at my parent's home. We were going to inspect a home in Londonderry."

"What happened next?"

"He first told me to go and put on a short skirt, and I kind of looked at him funny. He said that part of the job was to look good for the client. He said that sex sells."

"Did you do this?"

"Yes, I went into my room and changed, and I got into his car with him to go to the Londonderry home."

"And this was Londonderry, New Hampshire?"
"Yes it was."
"Were you parents' home?"
"No they weren't."
"Was there anyone else in the car?"
"No there, wasn't."
"What happened on the way to the Londonderry house in the car?"
"On the way to the home in Londonderry, he told me that a sexy woman can divert a male client's attention and win business. He also gave me instructions on what to do at the client's home. I was to sit provocatively with my legs open and cross my legs. He also showed me how to sit and then he grabbed my skirt and lifted it up. He told me I should show a lot of leg. He also told me that I should bend over and show certain places so people would look at me."
"How long did you work for Mr. Anderson?"
"It didn't last for more than one day, I quit."
"Why was that?"
"Once we got back to my parent's house, it was dark and after we pulled into my parent's driveway, he began to fondle me. I then pushed him away and ran out of the car telling him that I would never work for him."
"What happened next?"
"After I ran in the house, he left. My parents were home and I told them what happened."
"After you told your parents, what did you do next?"
"My parents took me to the Methuen police station and we pressed charges against him after we spoke to detective Rayno."
"And what happened to those charges?"
"We were scheduled to go to court, but it was postponed after his wife was murdered, and after he was arrested for the murder of his wife, the charges were dropped."
"Thank you. No further questions."

****

Attorney Carney walked to the stand.

"Ms. Lopez, did anyone see your allegation that you were assaulted by Robert Anderson?"

"No. It happened quickly before I ran out of the car."

"Did you scream?"

"No. I just ran out of the car."

"So there were no witnesses to this assault?"

"No."

"And this never went to court."

"No."

"Thank you."

Judge Barton adjourned court for the day with instructions to both attorneys to be prepared for closing arguments the following day.

****

That night, the Eagle Tribune's headline read: "I didn't kill her."

****

When court resumed the following day, the prosecution gave its closing argument first.

The closing argument was given by Prosecutor McAlary. He went over each individual's testimony and how it implicated Anderson. He restated the facts of the case beginning with Amy's family and the inconsistencies in the timeline that would have prevented the Anderson's from going anywhere but directly to the Shawmut bank in Lawrence, and how Amy and Robert were recently arguing. He also elaborated on how it was a typical defense ploy to try and put the blame on someone else. In this case, William Prince, and how it was an act of desperation. McAlary also showed that Anderson was the only one who had access to the guns that were found with the murder weapons. McAlary was particularly meticulous on how he presented the blood splatter evidence and the transfer evidence from the ceiling tiles in Cherry and Webb to Anderson's jacket. There was much more circumstantial evidence in the form or the bloody key to Cherry and Webb found in Anderson's home. McAlary argued that the motive was obvious, Robert Anderson's love for Pam McEvoy and his love of money. McAlary then detailed how Anderson showed this love by showering her with gifts and money. As an additional motive, Amy was going to divorce Robert, and he did not want to split his assets.

McAlary stated, "That while most people in similar circumstances would divorce their wives, Mr. Anderson's love of money determined how he would get out of a tethering marriage, by killing his wife."

However, McAlary's last statement, too many, sealed the deal:

"Ladies and gentleman of the jury, you heard Robert Anderson's testimony. Please keep in mind, Robert Anderson's testimony was in direct contradiction to every other witness. So if he's telling the truth, every other witness is lying. Robert Anderson has every reason in the world to lie, the other witnesses do not. No matter how you look at it, all the evidence of this case points to Robert Anderson as the one who murdered his wife."

"Thank you."

Judge Barton called for a brief recess prior to Jay Carney's closing argument.

****

Jay Carney began his closing argument by stating that there is no direct evidence showing that Robert Anderson murdered the woman he loved. He stated that the government's case is nothing but "smoke and mirrors" built solely on circumstantial evidence. Carney argued that there is more than reasonable doubt that Robert Anderson did not kill his wife.

"As a matter of fact," Carney said, "there is just as much evidence to convict William Prince. Prosecutors twisted the evidence to make it consistent with their murder theory."

The thrust of Carney's closing arguments was that Robert Anderson did not have a motive for killing his wife, even if he did love his twenty-six year old assistant, that love was not returned. There was no reason for Anderson to kill his wife to take up with a woman who would not have him.

Carney went on to state that, "Yes, Robert flirted with Ms. McEvoy who was the 'Ice Princess.' Yes, he gave her gifts, but that doesn't make him a killer. Robert was going through a mid-life crisis, and while some middle-age men begin wearing an earring or grow a ponytail during this time, others, like Robert, begin to flirt with a woman twenty years younger trying to show that 'they still have it.'"

Carney then addressed Pam McEvoy's testimony concerning the night she and Anderson spent in a Worcester hotel room.

"Ms. McEvoy testified that Robert brought her to a hotel room with one bed during a training seminar. She said that she wanted her own bed, but when that didn't happen, she spent the night in street clothes. There was almost hilarious testimony about a grand seduction. The hotel room that night had the qualities of a Rodney Dangerfield skit. Mr. Anderson puts his hands on Ms. McEvoy, she bats them away and then says, 'get me my book.' What would Bob get by killing his wife? The answer is nothing."

"Thank you."

****

Judge Barton then gave closing instructions to the jury paying particular attention to the difference between first and second-degree murder as defined by Massachusetts law. Specifically, first-degree murder is the more serious conviction. For a person to be convicted of first-degree murder, the prosecution must prove beyond a reasonable doubt that the defendant: acted with intent to kill or inflict serious harm with malice, acted willfully and planned the murder in advance.

Second-degree murder is differentiated from first-degree murder because it lacks the element of premeditation. It occurs when someone unlawfully and intentionally kills another, but did not devise a plan to commit the murder. The killing is instead the result of unscheduled, willful and purposeful intent to harm another person, or an indifference to human life.

The judge then remanded the jury to deliberations.

Many were estimating how many days it would take the jury to reach a verdict and if it would be a hung jury.

Two hours and forty minutes later, the jury reached a verdict and everyone was instructed to return to the court room.

****

As the jury was walking back into the courtroom, Robert Anderson was overheard asking Jay Carney what a quick decision means. Carney answered, "It is either very good, or very bad."

As the jury sat down, the bailiff yelled, "All be seated." He then went to the jury foreman and was handed the jury's decision which he, in turn, brought to Judge Barton.

Judge Barton opened the envelope and read the decision. His face gave away nothing. He then addressed the jury foreman.

"Ladies and gentleman of the jury, have you reached a decision?"

"We have your honor."

"What say you?"

"Your honor, we have found Robert Anderson guilty of murder in the first degree."

The court erupted.

Judge Barton banged his gravel and called for order in the court and then addressed the defendant.

"Robert Anderson, this is one of the most atrocious murders I have ever sat on. Having been found guilty of murder in the first degree, I remand you to be transported to MCI Norfolk prison for the rest of your life, with no chance of parole."

Judge Barton then addressed the jury.

"Ladies and gentlemen of the jury, you are dismissed and thank you for your service."

"All stand," cried the bailiff.

Once the judge and jury left, the courtroom once again erupted.

When the jury foreman had announced his verdict, and the judge his sentence, Anderson's head dropped and his eyes were downcast. He then looked back up shaking his head while attorney Carney placed a hand on his back while talking in his ear.

Two Essex County Sheriffs approached Anderson, handcuffed him, and led him out of the courtroom. He had been staying at the Essex County house of correction since his arrest. Once out of the courtroom, they were now going to transport him to MCI Walpole, Massachusetts, a state run maximum security prison that had more stringent rules than the county run maximum security prison. As he was led passed his crying mother who was hugging his brother Harold, Anderson whispered, "I love you."

Anderson then walked past Detective Jack McDonald. They looked each other in the eye and Jack said, "Good luck Robert, you're going to need it." Anderson said nothing.

Anderson was then brought to the holding room in the courthouse where the deputies allowed his mother to visit him for thirty minutes. He was then taken first to the house of correction to get whatever belongings he had, and then Walpole.

Amy Anderson's family broke into tears of joys while hugging each other. Amy's bother stated to Eagle Tribune reporter Bill Murphy that, "My mom said that this was going to be bittersweet. No matter what happened here, Amy won't be coming back. We'll try to put this behind us, there are so many scars, but justice has been served."

Prosecutor Fred McAlary stated, "The cooperative efforts between Mass State police and Salem, NH and Lawrence police helped build a case on very persuasive circumstantial evidence. I have nothing but praise for all detectives involved. The verdict was appropriate. I'm just a little surprised they came in with a verdict in just under three hours given the more than one hundred and forty exhibits in the case."

When McAlary was asked how he felt about beating one of the best defense lawyers in the state, he was very gracious and had nothing but praise for Jay Carney. McAlary stated, "Jay Carney's closing argument was the best I've heard in my seventeen years as a prosecutor. He just didn't have the evidence and facts to work with."

Jay Carney said that Robert Anderson was "crushed and devastated" and continues to proclaim his innocence. Carney went on to say that his client received an extremely fair trial but does see the possibility of an appeal.

When jurors were interviewed, they stated that they found nothing believable in Robert Anderson's testimony. John Williams, the jury foreman, stated, "Although the testimony of the witnesses was taken into account, we based our verdict primarily on forensic evidence. It was a tough decision and you have to make it correctly. We're talking about a man's life. I went by the facts. We sat down and started deliberating right away. There was no disagreement among the panel members."

Williams went on to say that for some jurors, it was very emotional. "A lot of the jurors had a hard time comprehending how anyone could do anything like that, however, we never wavered during deliberations."

Juror Carl Capobianco was not impressed with Anderson's testimony. "He did it to save his own skin and the prosecutor said it well, 'if Anderson is telling the truth, every other witness is lying.' I've been on a jury before, and this was a good jury. No one talked amongst themselves."

Another juror stated, "This was a killing of extreme atrocity and cruelty. I won't lose any sleep tonight knowing Robert Anderson is going to prison for the rest of his life with no chance of parole. Hopefully, this is some comfort to Amy's family."

Authors note: The reader may have noticed that throughout the trial, the prosecution always referred to Robert Anderson as Mr. Anderson whereas the defense referred to him as Robert or Bob. The purpose of this by the defense was to personalize the defendant and gain juror empathy. This clearly was to no avail in this instance.

The difference between a maximum and medium security prison is that a maximum security prison holds the most heinous criminals. These inmates have a violent criminal history or have committed violent crimes while incarcerated. These inmates need the most security and pose a threat to other inmates, prison guards, and society as a whole. Maximum security prisons are reserved for those prisoners who have committed the most serious crimes such as murder, robbery, kidnapping, treason, or other serious crimes who are serving long sentences and are an ongoing threat. Their movements are restrained and they are allowed out of their cells only for limited times during the day. Many get fed in their cells and are escorted to the shower and bathrooms separately.

Chapter 10
Epilogue

Reporter Bill Murphy continued to burn the midnight oil. That Sunday, the Eagle Tribune ran a special article titled, "A Lesson in Betrayal." In this article, he interviewed William Prince, the person who the defense tried to place the blame for the murder of Amy Anderson.

William, "Billy" Prince said he is getting along with his life but remains wounded by Anderson's attempt to turn him into a patsy. "I used to look up to Robert Anderson," he said. "He was my teacher and then gave me a good job and responsibility. Then, he dragged my name through the mud. I don't think that's right. How will I ever trust anyone again? I don't have a word to describe what he did to his wife and then to me. There's got to be a better word than dirt bag."

"Robert Anderson was my role model. I'd work at a moment's notice day or night. I did all the dirt work. Basically, he knew that I could get things done. I was his main man."

Prince went on to say that Anderson gave him an incentive to work hard by casually inferring that at some point he could own his own cleaning franchise and that he may even sell him one of his four franchises.

Prince said, "He had the world at his fingertips. He had a beautiful home. He had a great business and business was booming. He had a great wife and two beautiful kids, and he threw it all away."

Prince always defended his ex-teacher and mentor concerning people referring to Anderson as a sexual predator and how he was actually guilty of assaulting a cheerleader in 1984.

"People would say things about him like he was a child molester. I would stick up for him and say 'he wouldn't do that.'"

Bill Murphy touched on the subject of Anderson's lawyers and how they tried to shift the blame on him for the killing of Amy Anderson.

"I don't know how they sleep at night," Prince said.

Andrew D'Angelo, one of Anderson's defense team, said, "Our duty was to provide the best defense possible for Robert Anderson. In a first-degree murder case, it's a lawyer's obligation to ascertain that the commonwealth proves every element of the crime beyond a reasonable doubt."

Prince was able to get a new job at a semi-conductor plant in Windham, and when asked what he would like to say to his former boss and mentor, he stated that he has not talked to Anderson, "But I may write him and say, 'don't you wish you were here?'"

****

Later on that week, it was announced that Robert Anderson lost a wrongful death suit brought forward by Amy's family. The Rockingham County Superior Court, in Exeter NH, at the time, ordered Anderson to pay 1.8 million dollars to his two daughters aged eleven and nine. Amy's mother and sister, were the co-guardians of the children and would be entrusted with the money.

The lawyer for Amy's family stated that the guardians will use the money from the fund to raise the Anderson children and for a college education.

One of the guardians of the Anderson's children, Amy's sister, said that the children took the verdict with hidden sadness. She said that they probably won't comprehend the tragedy until many years later.

****

In 1997, Anderson had a new lawyer, Roger Covey, who brought forward an appeal of Judge Barton's verdict to the Massachusetts Supreme Court. The appeal was based on two incidents; Judge Barton allowing Francesca Lopez to appear as a rebuttal witness for a sexual assault allegation that occurred prior to the murder of his wife, and allowing the jury foreman to remain on the jury.

In regard to the rebuttal testimony, the Massachusetts Supreme Court ruled the following:

Although the rebuttal testimony was collateral to the main issues of the trial, the evidence tended to cast doubt on the defendants credibility because it created a basis of doubt from which the jury might infer that because the defendant's testimony was not accurate in this instance, other portions of his testimony may also not be accurate. A judge in his discretion, may permit impeachment by extrinsic evidence on collateral matters. Also, the defense did not object to the prosecutors questioning of the defendant regarding other female "marketers."

We conclude that Judge Barton was correct in allowing the jury the benefit of rebuttal evidence which contradicted the defendant's testimony.

****

The second issue before the court was Judge Barton's decision to allow the jury foreman to remain as a juror after he informed the judge that he knew one of the witnesses from twenty-seven years in the past as a babysitter for his children.

The State Supreme Court ruled that Judge Barton properly determined that the juror's memory of the witness was faint at best. More importantly, the juror repeatedly and unequivocally indicated that he could, and would be fair and impartial and he was not impeded by any emotional or intellectual commitment.

We conclude that the judge carefully considered the issue and determined that the juror could be fair and impartial. Nothing in the record convinces us that there was an error of law or an abuse of discretion on the part of the judge.

The following is the conversation between Judge Barton and the jury foreman in his chambers where both attorney Carney and McAlary were present:

Judge: "I understand that you reported to the court officer that you recognized one of the witnesses yesterday?"
Juror: "Yes. After lunch I did recognize her. Originally, when you asked if we knew any witnesses, I said no, and I hadn't seen the girl for twenty-seven years, She used to babysit my children when she was a student at Merrimack College and I didn't recognize the name because that was not her name at the time."
Judge: "You knew her by her maiden name."
Juror: "Yes."
Judge: "Have you seen that woman in the past twenty-seven years?"
Juror: "No. I didn't recognize her until we came back from lunch. I said to myself, gee that looks like my old babysitter. But I still wasn't sure."
Judge: "Let me ask you this sir. Now that you know this was your babysitter twenty-seven years ago, would that

affect your ability to judge her credibility objectively just as you would a stranger whom you never knew?"
Juror: "No."
Judge: "Mr. Foreman, do you feel that you can completely put out of your mind the fact that this woman, twenty-seven years ago, was your babysitter and judge her credibility just as you would a stranger's?"
Juror: "Yes I do."
Judge: "I am satisfied that you will remain fair and impartial. I am ordering you sir, not to mention this to any other juror in this particular case because you are the foreman of the jury and will definitely be one of the deliberating jurors. I am telling you now sir, I am ordering you not to tell any other juror either before or during deliberations of your knowledge of that witness twenty-seven years ago and the circumstances under which you know her sir. I am confident that you will remain fair and impartial. Fair and impartial to the Commonwealth, and fair and impartial to the defendant."
Juror: "I will your honor."

The judge sent the juror out of the room and made the following finding to Carney and McAlary:

"I am satisfied not only on the basis of the words that I heard, while watching the demeanor of the individual, but I am also satisfied that he will bend over backwards to remain fair in this particular case and so, under the circumstances, and exercising my discretion, based on the answers I've heard, and the behavior and mannerisms of the individual, I feel that he is, and can be, fair and impartial.

****

Narcissism, a love of women and money, and extreme arrogance were all traits shared by Stuart, Simpson and Anderson, and these were the traits that led to their downfall. I have no sympathy for any of them.

Chapter 11

Where Are They Now

Robert Anderson is 72 at the time of this writing and since his appeal, he was transferred from MCI Walpole, a maximum security prison to MCI Norfolk, a medium security prison. He is not considered a flight risk or a danger to others. He stays in touch with friends and family and still professes his innocence. There have been no other appeals, to the author's knowledge, since 1997.

****

Judge Robert Barton faced mandatory retirement in 2001 at age 70. He was one of the most respected superior court judges in Massachusetts. At the time of his retirement, the court cases he overseered had the least amount of reversals by the state Supreme Court. He was asked to audition for the television program Divorce Court, however he didn't get it because they were looking for a "Judge Judy" type person.

Barton remained in the public eye after retirement. He was the legal analyst for channel 5 where he made weekly appearances on TV.

Barton lives in the same house he and his wife have occupied for fifty years in Bedford, Ma.

****

Judge Robert Marshall was the most loved judge in Salem's history. He was considered a no-nonsense cop's judge and was harsh on criminals. However, he was demanding of "his" police officers. He was instrumental and the driving force in the construction of the Salem, NH District Court House.

He unfortunately had a forced retirement in 1998 at age 70, (NH Law) and retired to Florida with his wife Helen, where he passed in 2004.

****

George Phillips retired from the police department in 1998 and accepted a position in the Rockingham County Sheriff's Department until he retired as a Sergeant in 2012. All three of his children work in law enforcement with one who is currently a Chief of Police, another who is a Deputy Chief, and the third is retired.

He lives with his wife of over 50 years in Salem, NH and dotes on his grandchildren.

****

Detective Beaudet retired in 2005 after working for the Salem Police Department for 25 years. He then went to work for eight years as an armed guard for the Andover IRS. He is now fully retired and lives in Florida with his wife. He occasionally tries his hand at golf.

John Tommasi has suggested that he take up fishing instead.

****

Fred Rheault successfully worked on a number of homicides over the years including the double murder of two teenage girls at Hedgehog Park in 1997. He retired from Salem in 2008 after twenty-five years as a Lieutenant. He then worked at the University of Massachusetts in Lowell for four years and then moved to Hampton Beach with his girlfriend where he now works for the US Postal Service.

****

Jack McDonald retired from Lawrence PD in 2001 after thirty years. He spent eighteen years in homicide. He currently lives in Dracut, Ma with his family.

****

Trooper Norman Zuk continued working for Massachusetts State Police for thirty-four years. In 1996, he was promoted to Sergeant and worked the anti-terrorism squad at Boston's Logan Airport. Within several years he was promoted to lieutenant and was given control of the detective unit in 2009 where he continued to work major homicides. While still a Trooper, he passed away in 2018 from complications of a bone marrow transplant.

****

Bill Rayno retired from Methuen PD in 1996 but continued to teach at Northern Essex for another five years. For the next 10 years he was the head of Security at the Methuen Mall before retiring for good.

In 2021, at the age of 86, he and his wife of 60 years died in their house in Methuen from carbon monoxide poisoning as a result of a faulty boiler.

****

Bill Simone retired shortly after Bill Rayno. He served in the Methuen Police department for over thirty years, retiring as a lieutenant. He was also a U.S. veteran having served in the U.S. Army. William was the recipient of the AFEM Medal, the SPS Rifle Medal the Expert M-14 Rifle Medal and the Vietnam Service Medal. He died from natural causes in 2018 at the age of 71.

****

J. W. Carney continues to practice law out of Boston, Ma. He is the head of J.W. Carney and Associates. He has been rated as one of the top five attorneys in Boston by Boston Magazine. He has defended such high profile defendants as crime boss and fugitive James "Whitey" Bulger, Tarek Mehanna, the American pharmacist convicted of conspiracy to provide material support to al Qaeda, and John Salvi who was an abortion opponent who carried out fatal shootings at two abortion facilities in Brookline, Massachusetts on December 30, 1994.

****

Fred McAlary continued as the prosecutor for Essex County until he began his own practice in Andover, Ma. He is currently retired and living with his family in New England.

****

Mathew Stuart was paroled in 1995 and the conditions of his parole were terminated in 1997. Within the year though, Mathew was arrested for cocaine trafficking with two others, however, he was released and charges were dropped after three months. It has not been made public, but it was believed the charges were dropped because he turned state's evidence against the other two and set up a deal with his seller.

For the next ten years, he worked a number of menial jobs while suffering from alcoholism and cocaine abuse. On September 3, 2011, he was found dead in the bathroom of "Heading Home," a Cambridge, Ma homeless shelter. A subsequent autopsy showed that he died from "acute intoxication by the combined effects of ethanol and cocaine." No one in his family agreed to talk to the press, and the funeral, like his brothers, was sparsely attended.

****

OJ Simpson's trial did not end until Friday, September 29, 1995 at 3 PM. At that time, Judge Ito gave the final instructions to the jury and remanded the case to the jury at 4 PM.

The Jury began deliberations on Monday, October 2 at 9 AM. Like Robert Anderson's trial, the jury reached a decision in a very short period of time, four hours. However, unlike Robert Anderson, the predominately minority jury (eight blacks, three Hispanics and one caucasion) found OJ Simpson not guilty of murder or assault. Simpson was set free.

However, the saga of OJ Simpson was far from over. In a civil trial brought forth by the families of Nicole Brown Simpson and Ron Goldman, Simpson was convicted of a wrongful death and was forced to pay over $30 million in reparations to the families of Nicole Simpson Brown and Ron Goldman.

It is much easier to convict in a civil trial since only a preponderance of evidence is needed, whereas in a criminal trial, proof beyond a reasonable doubt is required.

One juror who sat on the civil trial stated, "Finding OJ Simpson liable of the murders, and acting with oppression and malice, was one of the easiest decisions I have ever had to make in my life."

More was yet to come.

In September of 2007, Simpson was arrested in Las Vegas and charged with numerous felonies including armed robbery and kidnapping. He was found guilty in 2008 and sentenced to 33 years in prison at the Lovelock Correctional Center in Nevada. He was paroled in 2017, and the conditions of his parole were terminated in October, 2021.

On January 2, 2022, Tampa Bay Buccaneers football player, Antonio Brown, had a temper tantrum for being benched, stripped off his shirt in the third quarter and walked off the field bare chested. In a YouTube video, OJ Simpson said that Brown's actions were inexcusable and he needs to control his temper.

OJ Simpson is currently 74, and lives in Las Vegas Nevada.

****

There aren't enough accolades or superlatives that can be given to the family of Amy Anderson. Her sister, brother-in-law and their two children, moved into the house at 187 Golden Oakes, and along with Amy's mother, raised Amy's children, as their own. The family shares a bond that many families can only hope to have.

****

There have been a number of scholarship funds set up in Amy's name in addition to a memorial tree that was planted at the High School by the Salem Garden Club.

One of Amy's students set up a web page dedicated to her titled, Rabbit, Rabbit, Rabbit and Amy Anderson. Some excerpts are as follows:

When I wake up on the first of the month I say "rabbit, rabbit, rabbit" to myself. I have been saying that one word three times on the first of the month since my sophomore year of high school, after hearing a story from my English teacher at the time, Mrs. Amy Anderson She said that it was something she did to have good luck.

The second memory is much darker. In late February of 1994 Mrs. Anderson was attacked while going out to get coffee for her husband who operated a cleaning business and was on a job site in Lawrence, Massachusetts.

It was later learned that Mrs. Anderson had been attacked by her own husband. Mr. Anderson was eventually charged with murder and found guilty.

The death of a teacher shook Salem High School and having been in her class made the entire event surreal. At the time I was in shock but I remember how odd it was to go to school the following Monday, sit in her old classroom and know that she would never be coming back to teach.

In recent years I have made a small addition to the superstition passed on from my 10th grade English teacher. After saying rabbit three times, I also say a little prayer for Mrs. Anderson and her family. May she rest in peace.

I hope you enjoyed this book. If you did, you may like another book I wrote;

Murder at the Front Door

It is the true story of the murder of Robert Cushing by off duty Hampton, NH Police Officer, Robert McLaughlin, who harbored a thirteen year grudge against Cushing. The following pages contain the prologue and part of Chapter one.

The book can also be obtained on Amazon.

Prologue

June 1, 1988 7 PM

Robert McLaughlin had just poured his third shot of vodka with a beer chaser. It was his fourth beer. He was sitting at the kitchen table of his small two bedroom apartment as he watched his neighbor, Robert Cushing Sr., get out of his car and walk into his house.

"Look at him, he has an ideal life, and I'm still a patrolman, all because of him. He doesn't deserve to be alive. It's because of him and his liberal son that I was never chosen for Detective or Sergeant."

****

December 12, 1955

Robert Randall and Fred Janvrin, both age 15, were best friends. After they came home from school they went to Janvrin's house in Salisbury, Ma, a border community with Seabrook, NH and a summer beach resort. Janvrin went downstairs to the cellar and came up with his father's 16 gauge, pump action shotgun and gave it to Randall who was at the top of the stairs. Unbeknown, to either teenager, the gun was loaded with double ought buck, 8 pellets with the approximate caliber of a .32, and the safety was off. Horsing around, Randall pointed the gun at Janvrin and pulled the trigger while saying "Pow." To his horror, the gun discharged with several pellets hitting Janvrin in the stomach and lower abdomen. After Janvrin fell down several steps and onto the cellar floor, Randall ran next door to a neighbor's house for help. The woman called 911 and then she and Randall ran back to Janvrin's house where she applied cold packs to Janvrin's head and tried to stop the bleeding. Janvrin was conscious at the time and Randall was hysterical and pleaded with Janvrin, "Not to die." In the follow-up investigation by police, Janvrin assured Randall that he would be okay and seemed to have no resentment about the shooting. Janvrin then became unconscious before the ambulance arrived, and died enroute to the hospital.

****

In a follow-up investigation by Salisbury police, the neighbor testified that she did hear the shot that killed Janvrin, but heard no yelling or any type of argument from the Janvrin home prior to the shooting. She also testified that Randall was highly emotional and collapsed after Janvrin was loaded into the ambulance. The parents of Janvrin expressed strong positive feelings towards Randall and stated that their son and Randall were the best of friends. They also stated that both boys never got into trouble despite the presence of several other boys with serious records living in the neighborhood. Police believed that both Janvrin and Randall hung out with the boys, but either did not participate in the trouble or were not caught.

However there was no doubt as to how upset Randall was over the death of his best friend. This was confirmed by the parents of both boys and Randall's teachers at school. This was not helped by boys at school who subsequently referred to Randall as "Killer" Randall for some time. He was also kidded by some delinquent boys that Randall, a murderer, was not going to prison while some of the other boys had done time in juvenile detention for less serious crimes, such as motor vehicle theft, kidnapping and robbery.

A Newburyport court judge ruled that that the shooting was a tragic accident and that Randall would do no time in juvenile detention but would undergo psychiatric counseling. A counselor determined that Randall was deeply troubled with survivor's guilt, and felt he had a need to be punished.

****

January 28, 1956

It was 5:40 PM when the boy walked into Dudley's Diner in Salisbury, Ma, about 1000 yards away from his home. He carried a double barreled shotgun that was not loaded.

"Is this a holdup," the waitress asked?"

The boy replied, "I guess so."

The waitress called another employee who recognized the boy and tried to talk him out of what he was doing. The boy told the waitress to give him the money in the register. She gave him $78. The boy replied that he only wanted half and gave her the money back. She counted out $39 and gave it to him. As he was leaving, one of the customers also tried to talk him out of it. The boy told the employees not to call the police until one-half hour after he left.

The boy went home, gave his stepfather the money, and told him that he wanted to turn himself in.

The waitress only waited 10 minutes before calling the Salisbury Police who went to the boy's house after responding first to the Diner. At the boy's house, they spoke to the stepfather and placed the boy under arrest.

Robert Randall had satisfied his need to be punished.

****

Robert was subsequently convicted of robbery in February, 1956 and went to juvenile detention where he underwent weekly psychological counseling. In August of that year, the courts and probation department received a report from Samuel Harder, M.D., of Boston, Ma. In this report, it was noted that Robert had spent two weekends home with his family and no difficulty was reported; quite the contrary, it was a happy weekend for all, including Robert's siblings. It was also noted that people in Robert's community harbored no ill will towards him, including the parents of Fred Janvrin. The report concluded with the Doctor stating that Robert had attained the maximum benefit from the counseling and would further benefit by returning home while being on parole/probation.

Robert was released and returned to school. He wanted to start anew which included taking the name of his supportive stepfather. He was subsequently adopted by his stepfather and changed his name to Robert McLaughlin after he was released from probation in February 1958, and went on with his life.

****

October 1973

Bob McLaughlin had been a police officer in Hampton, NH for 3 years and was one of three officers, two patrolmen and a Sergeant, on patrol during the midnight shift, when he received a call to respond to Punky Merrill's Gun & General Store in Hampton Falls, NH. Hampton Falls is a small town just south of Hampton, NH with a population of 2000. Its police department consisted, at the time, of a full time Chief of Police and four special (part-time) officers. When the burglary alarm at the gun shop activated, it went to the Rockingham County Sheriff's office who covered for part-time police departments in the county when no one was on duty. The county's deputies were tied up at the time and Hampton and Seabrook PD's were contacted. Seabrook advised that they would have someone available shortly. In Hampton, Patrolman Kennedy and the Patrol Supervisor, Jim Kerns, were busy on a domestic dispute call, hence, McLaughlin was the lone ranger responding to the burglary alarm.

As McLaughlin arrived at the gun shop, he noticed three men coming out the side door, all carrying bags. The owner of the store, Punky Merrill, lived in an apartment on top of the Gun Shop & General Store, and when he saw McLaughlin pull up, he came outside carrying his shotgun. McLaughlin got out of the cruiser with his shotgun which was loaded with number four buckshot. McLaughlin yelled for the three men to stop or he'll shoot. Up until the mid-eighties, it was legal to shoot a fleeing felon in NH. As the three men fled across the driveway towards the woods, McLaughlin took a knee and fired (at the time, burglary at night of an occupied structure was, and still is, a class A felony). McLaughlin aimed at the hardtop about three feet behind the burglar. He had learned at the firing range that when you fire a shotgun at the hardtop or cement, the pellets would bounce up six inches and continue on their trajectory at that height. Several of the pellets hit one of the burglars in the legs. He was later identified as Richard Carson.

"Headquarters this is 307, send backup, I have three burglars and shots fired."

By this time, Hampton's other two units were enroute to back him.

"Seabrook PD to Hampton, I have two units on their way to that location."

McLaughlin ejected the spent round, which also caused another round to load. After checking the guy who was wounded for weapons, he started to run after the other two. He heard shots and felt bullets whistling past him. As it turned out, after McLaughlin fired his shotgun, Punky Merrill opened fire with his shotgun. Fortunately for McLaughlin, Punky's shotgun was loaded with lead slugs that were still in the gun since the end of last deer season, if he had double ought or bird shot instead, it was quite possible that McLaughlin could have been shot by Punky. McLaughlin felt that one of the other two burglars fired shots at him but that was never proved.

Once he reached the woods, he stopped.

"Come on Bob, let's go after them," Punky said to McLaughlin. McLaughlin was a regular at Punky's store, like most local cops, they knew each other well.

"No, bad idea Punky, we got other units on the way, and if they see you with a gun, they may not recognize you and shoot."

"Yea, good point. I'll head back to the shop and turn on all the lights."

"Don't touch anything, we're gonna check for prints, and put the shotgun down."

"Gotcha."

When other units arrived they set up a perimeter and contacted State Police to see if they had a K9 unit available. Trooper Beaulieu, who was off duty at the time, arrived about an hour after the call and after a brief track through the woods, it ended at a dead end road where the burglars had probably left a car and subsequently fled.

The burglar who was shot, Richard Carson, was transported to Exeter hospital under guard. He was lucky. The one pellet that hit him went thru his calf without hitting any bone. He was released within 3 days and was eventually found guilty of burglary and sentenced to 2-4 years in county prison. He never gave up the names of his two accomplices.

However, John Paine was arrested after his fingerprints were found inside the store and he confessed. He also received 2-4 years in county prison. The third person was never found or identified.

Richard Carson subsequently sued the Hampton Police Department and Robert McLaughlin personally as a result of being shot by McLaughlin. To no surprise, this was a source of significant stress to McLaughlin which compounded the stress he was dealing with from the shooting. He firmly believed that he came close to dying. He was married and his wife was pregnant. The Town of Hampton's insurance carrier stated that since the shooting occurred in Hampton Falls, they weren't responsible and would not provide coverage to the Town on this incident. As a result, the Town of Hampton told McLaughlin that he was on his own and they wouldn't cover him. Fortunately for McLaughlin, the Hampton Patrolmen and Sergeants had just formed a union, and their lawyer, Whitey Frazier, later to become the Honorable Judge Frazier, threatened an unfair labor practice in addition to suing the Town civilly. The Town eventually relented and provided legal counsel and monetary coverage to McLaughlin. The lawsuit brought by Carson was eventually dropped, but the entire event had left Bob McLaughlin significantly scarred. He received a commendation for bravery. It was given to him in the locker room one day before roll call. It didn't help.

****

April 29, 1974

It was 11:32 PM on a warm evening in May.

"Headquarters to 308."

"Ten-three," Robert McLaughlin answered.

"Go to 942 Woodland Ave, report of shots fired and a man down on the front lawn. Ambulance enroute."

Holy shit Robert McLaughlin thought and then answered, "ten-five."

"Headquarters to 312, can you back him?"

"Ten-five, responding code 2," Rick Mathews answered.

"Three-oh-five copied also, I'll be responding." Car 305 was supervisor, Bill Ritchie.

"Headquarters to units, the ambulance will stage down the street from 942 and will respond once the scene is secured."

Four minutes later Bob McLaughlin arrived at the call.

"Headquarters I'm out, I got a man down and another with a handgun."

Damn, Bill Ritchie thought, and he upped his response to code three. Rick Mathews did the same.

McLaughlin didn't think, he just reacted. He grabbed the cruiser shotgun and racked a-round in the chamber as he exited the cruiser and took cover behind the engine block.

"Drop the gun," he yelled to the man who was now standing over the body, "and put your hands on your head and walk towards me."

The man dropped the gun and started walking towards McLaughlin as Bill Ritchie arrived on the scene. Bill got out of the cruiser with his gun drawn. The shooter was later identified as Joe Williams who owned a bus company. While McLaughlin covered Williams, Bill handcuffed him.

"Three-oh-five to headquarters, have the ambulance respond. We've secured the scene and have one in custody. Tell the ambulance to step on it, the guy who's down is covered in blood."

"Ten-five."

Mathews arrived at the same time as the ambulance, and accompanied them to the man lying in blood. He was later identified as Robert Muller from Lexington, Ma.

The first EMT to arrive took one look at Muller and said, "He's gone."

"How do you know?" Mathews asked.

"The bullet hole right between the eyes has something to do with it. That gray stuff oozing out of his head is his brains. Not a thing we can do."

At this time, Katherine Williams, Joe's wife, came out of the house screaming.

Mathews and McLaughlin were able to take her into the house and calm her down. Detective Sergeant Norm Brown arrived on the scene and covered the body with a blanket that was in his unmarked car. The other patrolman on duty was Jim Tuttle who arrived on scene shortly after Brown.

"Jim, this is Joe Williams, he's under arrest for murder, transport him to the station and book him. It'll be McLaughlin's arrest," Bill Ritchie said.

"That the dead guy on the steps?" Tuttle asked.

"Yup, deader than a door nail, got him right between the eyes."

"That's cold," Tuttle answered as he was putting Williams in the cruiser.

Both McLaughlin and Mathews were able to calm Katherine Williams down and she was able to call her sister to come get her.

While they waited, they were able to get most of the story from her. Joe and she were going through a nasty divorce that just got nastier, and they were separated. At some point, Joe drove by the house and saw Muller's car in the driveway. Joe suspected Katherine was having an affair. Katherine surmised that Joe parked his car down the street and shot Muller when he came out of the house.

After Katherine's sister arrived, McLaughlin walked her to the car from the side door so she didn't have to see the body. He then came back to see Ritchie.

"Okay Bobby, you have the arrest. Tuttle transport Williams back to the station and dicks are processing the scene."

"Ok Sarge, I'll start right on the report."

"And Bobby, good job."

"Thanks."

It was McLaughlin's second gun incident in eight months.

Back at the station, Williams had already confessed to then Hampton Police Chief Clayton Bosquin who had been contacted earlier. Bosquin relayed the confession to McLaughlin.

"Williams said he and his wife had been separated and began seeing a marriage counselor in recent weeks, but that Muller continued to see William's wife. Williams said friends and neighbors told him that Muller would come to the Woodland Road home after he had left for work."

Bosquin continued, "Williams then said after visiting with a friend, he drove by his house at around 11 when he saw Muller walking out the front door. He was holding the gun in his hand and pointing it at Muller's shoulder when Muller grabbed his hand and the gun went off. He didn't mean to shoot him, it was an accident."

After McLaughlin finished the report, he went home. It was 4 AM and he was still wound up from the night's incidents. He started drinking vodka with beer chasers.

McLaughlin was still drinking when Beverly, his wife, got up at 7 AM that morning.

"What the hell are you doing up and why are you drinking."

"I couldn't sleep. I went to a murder scene last night. Guy was shot right between the eyes. I saw his brains oozing out."

"I don't want to hear that. I'm making breakfast for Bobby junior. Deal with it and don't go talking to anyone at work. You don't want to lose your job. At least you got some overtime out of it."

Bob just looked at his wife. He went to bed and didn't get up until 5 PM that night, just in time to get ready for his 6-2 shift. He held everything in and didn't talk about it to anyone. The stress mounted for Robert. He received another commendation for his actions that night. This time it was in the roll call room.

****

Joe Williams was released the next day on $25,000 Surety bail. In other words, he put his house as collateral and walked out of jail. William's attorney, Richard Leonard, presented a letter to the court during a sanity hearing from a Boston psychiatrist who had examined Williams. Leonard quoted the doctor's letter as saying "Williams is not psychotic and not dangerous to himself and others."

His case went before a Grand Jury in June where they found no probable cause and the shooting was in fact an accident.

Charges against Joe were dropped and he and Katherine were eventually divorced.

****

August 17, 1975

Twenty-two year old Tim Campbell had just bought his Datsun 260Z and he couldn't believe how well it handled. It was a warm night and he had the T-tops off. What made it better was the gorgeous blonde, Paula, that was next to him in the passenger's seat. The night had gone well and as he was driving her home. He was hoping that she would invite him in. He was going a little too fast in his haste to get her home when he began to skid around a corner on Winnacunnet road. He overcompensated, began to fishtail and ended up in the oncoming lane. Luck was not with Tim and Paula that night. He hit a Dodge Swinger head-on as it was travelling in the opposite direction. Neither had their seatbelts buckled and both he and Paula hit the windshield. If anything good could be said, they died instantaneously.

****

"Headquarters to 307, respond to the area of 795 Winnacunnet Street for a 10-25 with PI, ambulance is enroute."

"Roger that headquarters, I'll be responding code 2," answered patrolman Robert McLaughlin.

Bobby, as he was called by his friends, had been on the Hampton, NH Police Department for five years. He was on his way to a serious motor vehicle accident with personal injury and he was going with blue lights and sirens. It was just before midnight.

"I copied that also, and I'll back him," stated then patrolman Rick Mathews. Rick and Bobby both got on the police department in 1970 and soon became close friends.

When Mathews and McLaughlin arrived at the accident site, they realized immediately that the accident was more serious than what the dispatcher indicated. It was a two car head on collision. They called for additional officers. They were joined by detective Tuttle and officer's Kennedy and Ritchie.

"Headquarters to units at the accident scene, two ambulances are enroute."

"Be advised," Rick Mathews responded, "we may not need them. This is a possible double 10-26," which was police code for a fatal accident. Rick called for additional units. Bill Wrenn, who was on a little more than a year, was one of the first units to arrive and he was immediately assigned to traffic control.

When the Hampton ambulances arrived on the scene, they confirmed the worst, it was a double fatal. They also called for a pumper truck to stand by as there was a gasoline leak from one of the cars involved in the accident.

The accident occurred in front of 795 Winnacunnet road, the Cushing residence. After being woken by the crash and subsequent arrival of emergency vehicles, Robert Cushing Sr. dressed, lit a cigarette and went out his front door to see what was going on.

He walked to one of the victim's car while smoking and was advised by officer's Kennedy and McLaughlin to leave the accident scene and put out the cigarette since there was gas leaking from the cars.

"Oh, because you have a badge you can tell me what to do? I live here," replied Cushing.

McLaughlin stepped up and stated to Cushing, "Sir, if you don't put out that cigarette and move back, you'll be placed under arrest."

"You can't arrest me."

"I can and I will. Last warning sir. Either move or you'll be in handcuffs."

With that said, Cushing begrudgingly moved off the road to his front yard.

A short time later, detective Tuttle began taking pictures of the accident. Cushing who was still steaming, from his recent encounter with McLaughlin, walked onto the road and in front of Detective Tuttle taking pictures.

"Sir, please move," said Officer Kennedy to Cushing.

"I will not move. You can't tell me what to do."

Officer McLaughlin was nearby. "Sir, you've been warned," and with that, officers McLaughlin and Ritchie placed Cushing under arrest and told him to place his hands behind his back.

"I will not. You can't arrest me."

A brief struggle ensued between Cushing and officer's McLaughlin and Ritchie. The struggle consisted of Cushing refusing to place his hands behind his back. After being assisted by Detective Tuttle, they were able to place the cuffs on Cushing and he was placed in the cruiser, transported to the station, and booked and bailed for disorderly conduct.

Bill Wrenn thought to himself that Cushing really tried hard to get arrested, and it appeared he succeeded.

When word of Cushing's arrest was circulated around town, everyone was amazed since they all felt it was out of character. He was a well-respected elementary school teacher. Cushing filed charges against the officers who arrested him and retained counsel to defend him. The charges against the officers were subsequently investigated and found to be without merit. There was eventually a negotiated plea to the disorderly conduct charge, which was continued for a year without a finding by Judge Gray at the District Court level. Essentially, a finding of continued for a year meant that if Cushing did not get arrested during the next year, the charges would be dropped.

****

September 23, 1975

It was a quiet Sunday morning in Hampton and 65 year old Gladys Ring was on her way to church when she rolled through a stop sign. Robert McLaughlin was on duty that day and was sitting on the side of the road observing traffic when Gladys went through the stop sign. After he pulled her over, Rick Mathews responded to back him.
"What do you have Bobby," Rick asked?"
"She blew a stop sign and she's upset that I stopped her. She won't give me her license." Both officers then approached the car.
"Mrs. Ring, if you don't give me your driver's license, we have no other choice but to arrest you and tow your car," McLaughlin said.
"I'm on my way to church, you have no right to stop me. I'm a grandmother."
"Ma'am, last time, if you won't give me your driver's license, you're going to be placed under arrest."
"You can't arrest me, my taxes pay your salary."
"Ma'am, step out of the car, you're under arrest."
"I am not," and with that Gladys locked her arms while grasping the steering wheel.

McLaughlin then opened the driver's door to the car and tried to pull her out of the car.

"Rick, give me a hand here, get her hands while I pull her out."

Both officers were then able to muscle Gladys out of the car but not before ripping the jacket she was wearing at the shoulder seem. She was transported to the station and charged with disobeying a police officer and resisting arrest. She was subsequently released on PR (personal recognizance) bail. Gladys Ring was the next door neighbor of the Cushings.

In a very short time, the story of Gladys Ring spread throughout the neighborhood and reached the ears of Robert Cushing Sr. and his son Renny. The Cushing's were outraged since the Cushing children and others in the neighborhood referred to Gladys as "Aunt Gladys."

The Cushing's, with Robert's arrest last month still fresh in their minds, started a petition within days that circulated throughout the neighborhood and Hampton condemning what they called the "aggressive tactics of the Hampton Police Department". They also demanded the termination of officer's Rick Mathews and Robert McLaughlin. The Cushing's went as far to appear before the Hampton Board of Selectmen to air their grievances.

After an internal investigation, both officers were cleared of any wrongdoing, and the petition went nowhere.

It seemed that everyone soon forgot about the incident, everyone except for Robert McLaughlin.

****

May 1, 1977

John Tommasi was a part-time police officer in Salem, NH, and even though he was finishing his Master's Degree in Business Administration in another year at the University of New Hampshire, he was seriously considering a career in law enforcement. It would have been a pay cut from his job at AVCO corporation (which was subsequently bought by Textron), but he was single, and money wasn't his primary concern in life. Going to a job he enjoyed was more important.

It was Sunday morning and he was doing fence duty at the construction site of the Seabrook, nuclear power plant. He was one of eleven Salem Police Officers who responded to the call for assistance from the Town of Seabrook. The newly formed Clamshell Alliance had over two thousand demonstrators surrounding the outside of the fence. They were anti-nuclear and their intent was to shut the site down.

Opposing them were two hundred and seventy police officers from all over New England. On fence duty with Tommasi was experienced NH State Trooper, Chris Colletti.

Looking at the demonstrators outside the fence, Tommasi said, "Hey Chris, doesn't this kind of remind you of the Alamo."

After a moment's hesitation Colletti turned to Tommasi and said, "Hey kid, ain't gonna fucking end like the Alamo."

"Good to know," Tommasi said nodding his head.

Later on that day, officers stationed at the Seabrook plant arrested over 1400 demonstrators in a mainly peaceful confrontation. Later on in life, Tommasi often wondered if Renny Cushing was one of the demonstrators he arrested.

****

April 1980

Bill Lally was a recent grad from Mt Wachusett College and he had just landed his dream job. He was a newly appointed patrolman in Hampton, NH. It was his third day on the job and he would be with a training officer for about four weeks. Today he would be working the 7 AM to 3 PM shift with newly appointed Sergeant, John Campbell. There was the usual roll call banter where new guys were the butt of the jokes and the banter. The logic being, if you're thin skinned and can't take the roll call hazing, you certainly wouldn't make it on the street. All this hazing in the locker room and rollcall was referred to as the "Murderer's Circle" by Hampton Police Officers.

After roll call, John introduced Bill to Bob McLaughlin who was just coming back to work from two days off.

"Glad to meet you Bill. How do you like it so far and when are you going to the academy?" Bob asked.

"It's great! I have a lot to learn and it looks like I'll be going to the academy at Pease Air Force Base in September."

"Well, you'll certainly learn a lot this summer. Hampton's population swells to over one-hundred thousand on some days, especially weekends," McLaughlin said.

"That's what I hear."

"Okay, enough of this, get in the car Bill, you're driving and your Sergeant wants a coffee," Campbell said kiddingly.

"Right Sarge. Nice meeting you Bob."

"You too Bill and good luck."

One of the things that Bill noticed was how immaculate McLaughlin's uniform was and he mentioned it to Campbell.

"His uniform was perfect. How does he get his boots like that?"

"It's called a spit shine. You'll have to learn that before you go to the academy. If not, plan on doing lots of pushups."

"Thanks. The Police Academy was recently increased to six weeks," Lally said.

"Yea I heard, when I went in 1974, it was only four weeks."

"Why is the academy at Pease?"

"They have army barracks that you stay in and cafeteria facilities. They'll be building a new academy in Concord, but it probably won't be ready until eighty-two. And by the way, the barracks are drafty, so you're lucky you not going in the winter, and the food sucks. On the plus side, you get to come home on weekends," Campbell answered.

"Got it."

"And by the way, if you want to model yourself after anyone, it's Bob McLaughlin. His uniform is always impeccable, and besides his shoes, he shines his brass every day. He's proud of the way he looks and the job he does. He's a real cop's cop, and his nickname is the Mongoose."

"Why's that?"

"Because like a mongoose, he always gets his quarry. He is relentless if he's investigating a crime, and his DWI reports are spot on. He's been in shootouts and high speed chasers and murder scenes. He has never lost a high speed pursuit and he's probably the best driver and shot in the department. He is the man"

"Thanks sarge, and that's not the first time I've heard that."

"Okay, coffee Lall."

Throughout his career, Lally was known as Lall.

****

Summer 1983

John Tommasi had been on Salem, PD for four years full-time, and was recently promoted to Patrol Sergeant. He had just started a business, Sub Sea Salvage, where he taught and certified Suba Divers and did underwater salvage work. After certifying eight members of the Salem, NH Fire Department, they were doing additional training with him on search and recovery.

Today, Tommasi was freelancing for an insurance company. He was diving in the Merrimac River recovering stolen cars that were driven off the boat ramp in Lawrence, Massachusetts, just north of the dam. There were two gangs in Lawrence that were responsible for the stolen cars, The *Southside Kings* and *License to Steal*. They would typically steal a high performance car, try to get in a pursuit with any of the local police departments, including Salem, NH, and then drive them off the boat ramp into the murky waters of the Merrimac River. Some gave Lawrence the unflattering moniker of stolen car capital of the United States.

Tommasi knew that the Merrimac was heavily polluted and over fifty thousand gallons of raw sewage was dumped into the river daily from Manchester and Nashua, NH. The EPA was just beginning to take measures to clean the river. In order to safely dive in the river, Tommasi had gotten a tetanus and gamma goblin shot to protect him from hepatitis A. He was also wearing a dry suit and full face mask.

This was Tommasi's first car he was diving on and he wasn't surprised that he had zero visibility. He located the car by the oil slick that was rising from the engine, followed it down 15-20 feet and attached the hook from a tow cable to one of the axles of the car. After surfacing, he would signal the tow truck driver who would winch the car out. He recovered sixteen cars that summer.

He was off that day and that night he spent at his beach cottage that he rented that summer on M street in Hampton with four other Salem cops who were all recently divorced. Tommasi, at thirty, was the only one who was still single. They were sitting on the farmer's porch at 11:30 PM, on the front of the cottage, when they were joined by Bob Mark, Bill Wrenn and Bob McLaughlin who just got off duty from Hampton.

"Hey, we heard you guys are having a choir practice," Bill Wrenn said.

"Yes we are," answered Tom Ferris one of the recently divorced Salem cops.

"And we have plenty of choir books for you guys too," said Mark Cavanaugh who was also recently divorced. Bottles of beer were passed around.

"Hey Tommasi, I heard you were diving in the Merrimac today," Wrenn said.

"Yea, I was contacted by an insurance company to recover stolen cars in Lawrence."

"No shortage of those. How's the visibility?" Bob Mark asked.

"What visibility? I literally couldn't see my hand in front of my face. There's shit floating everywhere in that river, and once I stepped on the bottom, my foot sank a foot into the silt"

"I hope they're making it profitable."

"That they do. I'm getting $100 for each car. Today was my first and I've got another dive scheduled in a couple of days."

"Doesn't Lawrence use the Merrimac for drinking water?" McLaughlin asked.

"Yea they do. They must purify the hell out of it. But I'm not drinking it."

"Now that you mention it, I won't either." McLaughlin said. The fact that the Merrimac was highly polluted and silted stayed with McLaughlin over the years. *Authors note: When cops get together after work and have a few drinks, it's known as choir practice. The bottles are referred to as choir books, and of course, the cops who are drinking, are called choir boys. It is believed that this practice was started in LA and was made popular by Joseph Wambaugh's 1975 book, The Choir Boys.*

****

April 5, 1986

It was the 1st week in April and the busy summer season in Hampton was beginning. April and May could be busy months depending on the weather, especially on weekends and it was an usually warm Saturday night in Hampton. Some people were taking long weekends and some of the college kids who had summer jobs in Hampton were beginning to show up.

Joe Galvin had just finished his rookie year and was glad to be off probation. It was 9 PM and Joe was sitting in his cruiser at the intersection of Ocean Blvd and Ashworth Ave, referred to as AshCor by members of the police department. He was watching both pedestrians and vehicular traffic. It was a fairly busy Saturday night when he heard a general announcement from dispatcher Mary Jo Ganley.

"Headquarters to all units, be on the lookout for a dark colored, older model Oldsmobile, with possibly Maine license plates, traveling north on Ocean Blvd from O street. One male subject driving, possible 10-19," 10-19 being police code for driving while under the influence.

Joe heard the call.

"Headquarters this is 306, I'm at AshCor and I'll keep a lookout for it." AshCor was about one-half mile north of O Street on Ocean Blvd. Ocean Blvd was a two lane road with one way northbound traffic. Ashworth Ave was for southbound traffic. Ashcor was the where the two roads became adjacent to each other.

Within minutes, Joe spotted the car.

"Headquarters, this is 306, I have a car and driver matching that description travelling north on the Blvd. I'll be stopping him."

"Headquarters to units, anyone in the area for backup."

Robert McLaughlin was in the station. He had just finished cleaning his handgun. In 1986, Hampton Police, like most other departments in New Hampshire carried the Smith & Wesson .357 magnums as a sidearm and every cruiser had a shotgun with double ought buck for ammo.

"Headquarters this is 308, I'm just clearing the station. I'll head that way." The police station was about ¼ mile from Joe's location.

"Headquarters, I'm attempting to stop that vehicle northbound on Ocean Blvd, he isn't speeding up, just not stopping, speed about 35. Be advised, he's all over the road," Joe Galvin radioed as he caught up to the Oldsmobile.

Upon hearing this, McLaughlin activated his blue lights and siren attempting to close the gap.

Rick Mathews, a recently promoted Sergeant was the supervisor that night.

"Headquarters, this is 305, I'm on Winnacunnet Rd east of the high school. I'm heading that way." Winnacunnet road was north of Joe's position and intersected Ocean Blvd.

"Headquarters this is 306, I have him stopped at the Century motel. He pulled into the driveway." The Century was on a section of Ocean Blvd referred to as Rocky Bend and had a horseshoe driveway with individual units lined around the drive. Joe had the car stopped in front of the second unit on the right. He parked his cruiser at an angle to the stopped Oldsmobile to offer some protection as he was taught at the academy.

"Joe, I'll be there in a minute," McLaughlin radioed.

"Me too," Rick Mathews echoed.

As Joe Galvin approached the driver's door of the Oldsmobile, he was able to smell alcohol coming from the driver, later identified as Ken Woodward, a Viet Nam Vet.

"Sir, can I have your license and registration and why didn't you stop for me," Joe asked.

"I had the radio up loud and I didn't notice you," Woodward replied.

As Woodward was talking, the odor of alcohol became stronger and Joe noticed how his speech was slurred and eyes were bloodshot. All good indicators of a drunk driver.

Joe went back to his cruiser and ran Woodward for a valid license. He came back under suspension for a previous DWI conviction. Hmm, Joe thought, the best judge of future behavior is past behavior

As Joe was exiting his cruiser, he noticed the driver, the only occupant, bend down and either put something under the seat, or take something out, he couldn't tell. This is what most police officers refer to as furtive movements which instantly put Joe on alert. As he approached the stopped Oldsmobile, Joe unsnapped his holster and put his hand on his .357. When he reached the driver's door, he stood back forcing Woodward to turn almost 180 degrees.

As Joe was about to ask him to exit the car and perform some field sobriety tests, Woodward pulled a gun, a Ruger Bulldog .44 magnum with a 2 ½ inch barrel. As Woodward turned, he fired at Joe, missing him. Joe returned a shot which missed Woodward and lodged in the steering wheel column. Galvin and Woodward were about three feet apart. Galvin retreated to his cruiser and he radioed that he's in a gunfight.

The Bulldog has a 5 shot capacity and Woodward quickly emptied his gun shooting at Joe missing him with every shot. Joe returned fire, shot for shot, also missing Woodward, but he saved the last bullet in his revolver, he didn't know that Woodward's gun was empty. Woodward then backed his car around Galvin's cruiser at the same time McLaughlin arrived on the scene from the south and Mathews from the north.

McLaughlin and Mathews both exited their cruisers with shotguns. As Woodward backed out of the driveway and began to head north on Ocean Blvd, McLaughlin fired a shot through the rear window completely shattering it, and as he attempted to eject the spent cartridge, his shotgun jammed. All eight .32 caliber pellets missed Woodward.

Mathews had pulled into the other side of the horseshoe driveway and as Woodward drove by him, he fired his shotgun at Woodward through the front passenger's side window shattering it. Mathews was kneeling down and shot at an upward angle, all eight of his .32 caliber pellets missed Woodward, with most of them going through the roof of the Oldsmobile. All three officers got back in their cruisers and gave pursuit along with Officer Lee Griffen who arrived at this time and was behind McLaughlin.

"Headquarters we're in pursuit northbound on Ocean Blvd, multiple shots fired. Contact North Hampton and Rye," Mathews screamed over the police radio.

Woodard took off northbound on Ocean Blvd with all four officers in pursuit.

"My shotgun jammed. If we start shooting again I'll be on my magnum," radioed McLaughlin.

"Sarge if I have the shot, can I shoot," radioed Griffen who was still in his rookie year."

"Hell yes," answered Mathews.

The pursuit continued north on Ocean Blvd.

"Ok, he's turning onto High street from OB, he could be heading for route 101 or 95, contact NH State Police," Mathews advised dispatch.

"Already did sarge," answered Mary Jo.

"Mass State police has been advised also."

"We're coming up on route 1," continued Mathews. What's common in many police pursuits is that the lead pursuit car, which was Joe Galvin, concentrate on driving while the second car in the pursuit, Mathews, called in locations. Route 1, also known as Lafayette road was the main north-south road in Hampton. There was usually a traffic bottleneck at the intersection of High street where there were stop lights. Woodward blew through the red light almost causing an accident. All four cruisers had their lights and sirens on which gave motorists some warning as they went through the intersection.

In another mile, Woodward turned onto route 101 west and from there, route 95 south barreling through a toll booth with four Hampton units and one NH state unit following which was waiting for them at the toll. This was radioed to Hampton Dispatch by Mathews.

"Headquarters to units, be advised, there are two Mass state units at the state line, they're planning on doing a rolling roadblock to try and slow him down. They are monitoring us," radioed Ganley.

"Units copy. We're about ½ mile north of the state line doing around 80-100. He's all over the road," Mathews replied.

A rolling roadblock occurs when multiple police units get in front of the vehicle being pursued and slowly reduce speed thereby slowing the chase, while other units box him in from the side and back.

"We're coming up on the state line and Mass state units are moving."

Since there were only two units, Woodward slowed slightly before flooring the pedal getting by the Mass state units while sideswiping one in the process.

"He's by the state units and he hit one as he was passing it. Pursuit is continuing south on 95, we're just south of the 495 intersection," Mathews radioed.

As the pursuit continued southbound on 95, the Mass state units tried to get past Woodward, but every time they did, he attempted to swerve into them.

"Mass 517 to base, I just want to confirm, this subject we're chasing fired shots at a cop."

"That's affirmative 517," Mass State Police dispatch answered.

"Okay, once I get pass the Whittier Bridge, I'm ending this."

"Base copies"

Mass State Trooper Richards was a 10 year veteran of the state police and had been in his share of pursuits. Pursuit policies in the eighties in both Mass and New Hampshire were much less restrictive than current pursuit policies.

As Woodward went over the bridge, Richards pulled alongside of him on the left. Woodward tried swerving into Richards, which Richards avoided. Richards responded by hitting Woodward's left rear quarter panel with the front right fender of his cruiser causing Woodward's car to spin out of control onto the median strip. Woodward tried running away, but was tackled. He resisted, was eventually subdued after a struggle, placed in handcuffs and transported to Newburyport, Mass PD. He was subsequently extradited to NH for trial where he was found not guilty by reason of insanity and sentenced to the state mental hospital. He was not released until 2017. All officers and Troopers involved in the shootout and subsequent pursuit received commendations and returned to work.

Another shootout added to McLaughlin's stress lever. A counselor that he had seen as a teenager once told him that lifetime stress was cumulative.

Chapter 1

Murder in the Neighborhood
Wednesday, June 1, 1988

Detective Bill Lally was now an 8 year veteran of the Hampton Police department and was watching the Celtics playoff game against the Detroit Pistons when he got the call from Dispatcher Fred Ruonala around 8:45 PM.

"Bill there's been a homicide at 795 Winnacunnet Street, they need you there."

"Did you say a homicide?" Bill replied. In his eight years as a Hampton police officer, there had not been a single murder, and the only time officers had to deal with a dead body during that time was usually a result of a car accident or untimely death.

"Yea, that's right, it looks like two shotgun slugs to the chest. Guy died on the spot. His name is Robert Cushing," Fred responded.

"On my way."

Bill told his wife Sandy where he was going, kissed her goodbye, and was out the door

The Cushing family was known to Bill and most of the Hampton Police Officers. Robert Sr. was well known in the Community, and Bill was aware that Cushing had previously been arrested for disorderly conduct. He also knew of his son Renny (Robert Jr.) Cushing who tried to get Rick Mathews and Bobbie McLaughlin fired for the arrest of Gladys Ring. He, and other officers, had also been to the Cushing house a number of times on loud party calls. There were seven children in the family and they were never really excited to see the police, especially given their father's previous interaction with the police.

Bill arrived at the house after first getting his gear at the police station and parked his cruiser adjacent to the yellow crime scene tape. As he walked into the house, he noticed two large bullet holes in the screen door and an enormous pool of blood coagulating on the inside hallway.

The victim, Robert Cushing, had been taken to Exeter Hospital via ambulance. He was very obviously dead at the scene because of blood loss and internal organ damage from two massive holes in his chest and abdomen, but because his wife was hysterical by that time, they felt it best that they transport him.

From the size of the holes in the screen door, Bill knew that they had to come from two shotgun slugs. He then noticed that there were no spent cartridges on the floor or outside the front door. After asking the uniformed officers present if they had seen any spent cartridges and getting a negative reply, he reasoned that the shooter had either policed his brass, or a double barreled shotgun was used which had to be broken open to eject the spent casings. Upon further observation, he saw no obvious clues. It was going to be a long night.

Authors note: Policing the brass is the phrase that is used to pick up spent cartridges after a gun is fired.

****

Fifteen minutes earlier

Marie Cushing, an avid basketball fan, was at home watching the Celtics playoff game like many people in the Boston area. Her husband, Robert, was across the living room sitting in an easy chair reading the newspaper while having a cocktail.

"I don't believe you're not watching the game," Marie said.

"You're the basketball fan, I'm enjoying just relaxing and being here with you," Robert replied.

"Come here and sit with me and watch the game. You can read the paper later."

As Robert got up to join his wife on the couch, there was a knock on the door.

"You're going to get that, right," Marie asked?

As Robert opened the front door, a momentary look of horror crossed his face as two blasts rang out through the still closed screen door driving the 63 year old Cushing back before he hit a hallway table. Marie screamed and rushed to her husband's side.

Coming in 2023
The true story of the murder of two teenage girls at Hedgehog Park in Salem, NH in 1997

Murder Outside the Bathhouse Door

The following is an excerpt from the Prologue

Prologue

From the Movie Scream/1996

Billy looked at his friend. "Now, Sid, don't you blame the movies. Movies don't create psychos. Movies make psychos more creative. We all go a little mad sometimes."

****

September, 1997

Detectives Beaudet and Sambataro were interviewing Eric Jeleniewski at the Salem, NH Police Department …

Jeleniewski was recounting the murder of 18 year old Kimberly Moore (pseudonym) at Hedgehog Park.

"I loved the feeling of her warm, sticky blood flowing through my fingers," Jeleniewski said.

Sambataro's shoulder and back muscles involuntarily contracted. He had a daughter Kimberly's age. Sambataro got up and shut off the video camera and then turned towards Beaudet, "Roger, go get a cup of coffee."

****

Murder On the Orient Express

Hercule Poirot, the world renowned detective, was traveling on the elegant Orient Express and accompanied by his friend M. Bouc. The train was unusually crowded for this time of year and a large winter storm was brewing.

While on the train, Poirot was approached by the mysterious millionaire, Mr. Ratchett. He wanted Poirot's protection while on the train and was willing to pay him handsomely to protect him, since he was receiving death threats. Poirot refuses since he sees Ratchett as a man of low character and ill repute. The train, that evening is stopped and stranded by a large snowdrift. Over dinner, Poirot notices some strange occurrences amongst the passengers on the train

During the night, Poirot is awakened by a cry in the night. When the conductor checks the room of M. Ratchett, a voice from the room states, "Ce n'est rien. Je me suis trompé." The conductor assumes this is the voice of Ratchett and all is well.

The following day, while the train is still stranded, Bouc informs Poirot that Ratchett has been murdered and the murderer is still aboard, having no way to escape in the snow. As there are no police onboard, Poirot takes up the case.

With the help of Dr. Constantine, one of the train's passengers, Poirot examines the body of Ratchett after his locked stateroom is opened by the conductor.

The Doctor is troubled. There are inconsistencies in the stab wounds, twelve of them. Some are severe and any one of them could have been the cause of death. Some of the stab wounds are superficial and barely puncture the skin.

Some of the wounds did not bleed, signifying that they were delivered post-mortem, after Ratchett had died.

And finally, at least one of the wounds were delivered by a person that was left-handed.

Poirot wonders, did the murder, (murderers?), leave the room and then return to make sure the deed was complete?

"What other explanation can there be?" Dr. Constantine asks.

In Poirot's words to Dr. Constantine:

"That is what I am asking myself. Some of these blows point to a weakness, a lack of strength or determination. Some are feeble glancing blows. But this one here, and this one. Great strength was needed for those blows."

"Ah! C'est rigolo, tout ca!"

****

Made in United States
North Haven, CT
14 November 2022